MW01145908

DIAMOND
ROCK

DIAMOND ROCK

by Mark Schorr

Author of
Red Diamond: Private Eye
and
Ace of Diamonds

St. Martin's Press
New York

DIAMOND ROCK. Copyright © 1985 by Mark Schorr. All rights reserved. Printed in the United States of America. No part of this book may be used or reproduced in any manner whatsoever without written permission except in the case of brief quotations embodied in critical articles or reviews. For information, address St. Martin's Press, 175 Fifth Avenue, New York, N.Y. 10010.

Library of Congress Cataloging in Publication Data

Schorr, Mark.
  Diamond rock.

  I. Title.
S3537.C598D5   1985 813'.52   85-2667
ISBN 0-312-19919-8

First Edition

10 9 8 7 6 5 4 3 2 1

To Bernie and Vera

PART ONE

PART ONE

Chapter One

The furniture in the lawyer's office was as worn as Diamond's temper. "We gonna keep going over the same ground all day? I don't have time to waltz you through it again."

"Mr. Jaffe, you will answer—"

"The name ain't Jaffe. It's Diamond, Red Diamond. I told you that a hundred times already. You got wax in your ears or what?"

The lawyer's face turned a bright red. He tugged the white hair at his temples. A blue vein throbbed at his forehead. A patriotic display, Diamond thought, as he shifted his glance to the doll in the corner.

She was good-looking, in a stuck-up sort of way, with a figure just full enough to give a guy something to hang on to. She was watching the lawyer like they had more than an attorney-client relationship.

She claimed to be Diamond's wife. Soon to be ex-wife.

He had never seen her mug before.

Her name was Milly Jaffe. At least that's what she said it was. Who could believe a dame who showed up out of nowhere saying she's a guy's wife, they got two kids, and she wants all his folding green?

Everybody knew his particulars, thanks to Scott

3

Marks writing those dime books and pulp potboilers. Red Diamond, who can outpunch Mike Hammer, outdrink Nick Charles, outsleuth Sam Spade, outshoot Race Williams, outwisecrack Philip Marlowe, outstud Shell Scott, outbench-press Spenser.

Everybody knew, except for Nichols the lawyer and the doll. Even the court stenographer taking the deposition knew the story. She looked so bored, she must've heard it before.

"I told you, he's crazy," Milly piped up. Her voice was like the caress of a broken beer bottle. "I want him committed. And I want what's coming to me."

"What's coming to you, sister, is a fat lip," Diamond said. "You're lucky I ain't the kind that believes in hitting a broad."

"Are you threatening to assault my client?" the lawyer said shrilly. "I'll get an injunction."

"You'll get the fat lip I owe her," Diamond said.

Milly jumped up. "See! I tried talking to him. He's nuts. He runs off and leaves me with two kids, nothing in the bank, a mortgage on a house that's ready to fall apart, so he can play cops-and-robbers."

She was nearly hysterical. "It was never easy, even with him home. He always had his nose buried in some dumb detective book, instead of going out and driving the cab so he could make—" She broke down. Nichols went over and put a consoling arm around her.

"Hearts and flowers time," Diamond said, mimicking playing a violin. "Joan Crawford meets Cesar Romero."

"That's it!" Nichols yelled. "We're not going for hidden assets, we're going for a commitment. To a nut house."

"Calm down, calm down, and start acting like adults," the other lawyer said. Diamond had almost forgotten him. They had met in the elevator, when Diamond was on his way up to Nichols's office.

4

"You're making an appearance without counsel?" he had asked.

"I'm going to this Nichols wisenheimer to find out how much of my juice this Milly dame wants."

"You could lose everything if you don't watch out."

"I been in tougher scrapes. One time, I was trapped in a mine shaft in Utah. Rocco had sicced a pack of wolves on me. I didn't have a roscoe. Couldn't even grab a piece of rock. My hands were tied behind my back."

The lawyer, who later told him his name was Moses Tartaglia, was amused.

"You heard this story before?" Diamond asked.

"I was an assistant D.A. in the Bronx for seven years. I've heard every story."

"So what happens?"

He thought for a moment. "You take off running, still they're gaining on you. You come to a big chasm and leap across. Then when the wolves try and jump after you, you wait on the other side and knock them into the pit. You're running and you see the car. You have to get away. So that's why you stole it. Guilty with an explanation, Your Honor. How's that sound?"

"That ain't the way it happened," the P.I. said. "But I like the way you think."

Tartaglia was a portly gent, balding, with bushy sideburns that looked glued to his cherubic face. His suit was cheap but freshly pressed. His shoes were made out of a substance resembling leather.

"I've got a case. I need an investigator who's a little offbeat. I'll come in and represent you with Nichols, you look into this for me. Deal?"

"How many cases have you handled?"

"Like I said, I was in the D.A.'s office for—"

"I mean, on the outside. As a defense attorney."

"Uh, well, this is my first week."

"And you hang around the halls looking to glom on to clients?"

"I'm no ambulance chaser," Tartaglia said indignantly. "I'm hiring you as much as you're hiring me. Quid pro quo."

"Ipso facto, habeas corpus, rigor mortis."

"Suit yourself. Go see Nichols. It's your funeral."

"Not a funeral. A divorce. Don't get yourself in an uproar," Diamond said, sticking out his hand. "We got a deal."

"There's no point in turning this into a shouting match," Tartaglia was saying.

"Listen, young man—" Nichols began.

"Don't patronize me, Nichols, or we'll walk out of here so fast it'll make your head spin."

Diamond grinned.

"What are you so happy about?" Milly demanded.

"Don't feel bad, cupcake. Nichols is doing the best he can."

"That's it, that's all the abuse I'm going to take," Nichols said, turning crimson again.

"Look at him go. He's redder than May Day in Moscow," Diamond said.

"I don't want to make this case my career," Tartaglia said. "We've been here an hour for what could've been done in fifteen minutes."

"That's because you have a lunatic for a client," Nichols snapped.

"Counselor, let me remind you of the laws regarding slander," Tartaglia said. "You are impugning my client in front of witnesses. Are you familiar with Sullivan versus—"

"I am very familiar with the case. Have you heard what your client has been saying this past hour? That he's

6

been a private eye since 1930, that he's worked with or knows every fictitious P.I., and that he's the best."

"Well, I wouldn't go that far," Diamond said modestly. "Just yesterday, me and Mike Hammer were belting back brews at Bogie's. We were comparing notes on—"

"He's bonkers. His name is Simon Jaffe. He's a cabdriver," Milly said. "He read stupid books about these ridiculous detectives and it caused brain damage. Not that there was much to be damaged."

Red felt the pounding in his head, like Gene Krupa going into a solo. He squeezed his eyes shut and then opened them. The scene was hazy.

"Do you want to step out in the hall and get some air?" Tartaglia asked. "You look pale."

"He's faking it! He's faking it to get out of settling with me," Milly said.

"We'll adjourn the proceedings," Tartaglia said to Nichols. "You and I can talk by phone, maybe work out something agreeable to both sides."

"You can't leave. I'll go to a judge and get a court order," Nichols said. "We'll have this hearing one way or another."

"Can the hot rhetoric, Nichols. I'd like nothing more than to take you apart in court. You want to do it the hard way, I'm ready. I'm sure Mrs. Jaffe will be willing to pay for the additional time. What are you making, sixty an hour?"

"Sixty? He's charging me a hundred," Milly said.

"And well worth it, I'm sure," Tartaglia said, getting up from the radiator he'd been slouching against. "C'mon, Mr. Diamond, let's leave these two to talk."

They took a couple of steps toward the door and Tartaglia turned to the stenographer. "I'd like a copy of this tomorrow. Suitable for framing."

7

"You were pretty good in there," Diamond said as they rode down together in the elevator.

"You were kind of weird."

"I don't know why, sometimes I get these headaches."

"Do you feel like talking over my case now?"

"Over a cup of java. My treat."

"Sounds fair. I know a place up the street where no one has died from eating their danish."

They found a vacant table in the back of the restaurant, brushed the crumbs off the chairs, and sat down. Diamond faced the door. Tartaglia began to set his briefcase on the formica tabletop, noticed the rainbow of stains, and kept it on the floor, clamped between his feet.

The yawning waitress hadn't recovered from the lunchtime rush. She moved slowly on tender feet and seemed annoyed when they only ordered coffee and a couple of turnovers.

"How'd you get a moniker like Moses Tartaglia?" Diamond asked as they waited.

"A mixed marriage. My father's Polish, my mother's Puerto Rican."

"You're sharp on the uptake," Diamond said. "That crack about rates threw a monkey wrench in his gizmo."

"That won't stop him from chewing us up if we have to go to court. Gimme a minute to review your divorce papers." Tartaglia turned his attention to the documents he'd picked up in Nichols's office.

Diamond studied the booths around them, where well-dressed men spoke in whispers. More deals were made in the hash house than hamburgers. Bail bondsmen, judges, court clerks, prosecutors, defense counsel, cops, probation officers—plea bargaining, fixing tickets, perfecting testimony, drumming up business.

It reminded Diamond of a time in Chicago:

The shop was a gavel's throw from the courthouse, filled with the usual types you find in the court system shadows. Hustling bail bondsmen, ambulance-chasing attorneys, cops who could be bought for the price of a lunch, and judges who cost at least a dinner.

I opened the door and let in a biting blast of Lake Michigan air. The joint could use it. It smelled of old cooking oil, stale cigars, and corruption.

I unbuttoned my trenchcoat and patted the roscoe slung under my shoulder. It was cold and hard, like the pavement where Bucky the newsboy lay. He was a good kid, caught in the mob's crossfire.

Rocco Rico was behind the lead. It was meant for me. I'd been lucky. Bucky hadn't been. A tough little thirteen-year-old supporting his crippled mother and blind sister.

The Right Honorable Richard T. Mallory sauntered in, full of legal pomp and circumstance. When not giving stiff sentences to teenagers who'd swiped a jalopy for a joy ride, he fixed cases for Rocco.

He took his time looking over the crowd, getting nods and waves from the regulars. Then he spotted my ugly puss and strutted over like we was old pals.

The coffee shop got quiet. A few of the Nervous Nellie types drifted out. A pair of harness-bulls unbuttoned their heaters. If Mallory got plugged, a key cog in the machine would be missing.

I checked my burger for ground glass.

"Can I sit down?" a smiling Mallory said. He didn't wait for an answer, plunking his judicial posterior down on the seat. "The food is quite good."

"It's rotten. Just like the creeps that hang out here."

I said it with a big grin, in a chatty tone, and it took Mr. Jurisprudence a moment to realize I wasn't chumming up to him. Then his smile disappeared faster than a reformer vote in a Cook County voting machine.

9

"Smart mouth you got there. Maybe I ought to have a few of the boys take you out and wash it with soap," he said, casually glancing back to where his bull buddies stood.

"Why don't you take a look under the table?" He slowly leaned over and looked. His eyeballs exploded like popcorn.

"Now I ain't claiming to be the best shot in the world. But I figure if I don't hit my mark at this distance, they oughtta yank my peeper's license and make me sell pencils on the street corner."

"What . . . what do you want?"

"You know that newsie that got shot?"

"An unfortunate tragedy."

"You bet. In keeping with the Christmas season, you're gonna make sure that Bucky's mom and sis are taken care of. The girl needs an operation, and I know a judge who suddenly wants to make like Santa Claus."

"That's extortion."

"Better call it blackmail. I got the shots of you and Rocco meeting. The Sun-Times and the Trib will splash them right on page one. It's terrible, these muckrakers, ain't it?"

He muttered and sputtered for a few minutes, but in the end agreed. Then I put the arm on him for something he really didn't want to give up—where Rocco was hiding.

"Calling planet Earth," Tartaglia's voice said, and Red snapped out of his reverie. "Do you hear me?"

The lawyer sat watching him, his cup drained, his plate empty. There was a hint of concern beneath his cynical tone.

"Sure, sure, I'm fine."

"What were you thinking about?"

"Something this scribbler Scott Marks wrote a while ago."

"You don't strike me as the literary type."

10

"I'm full of surprises. Besides, he wrote it about me. Anyway, what were we talking about?"

"We weren't. I was eating, and you were off touring the universe."

"So what kind of case you got for me? Murder, blackmail, kidnapping?" Diamond asked hopefully.

"It's a divorce case."

Diamond leaned back. "I don't do them. That's for sleazy peepers who like barging into by-the-hour motel rooms so they can catch John Q. Public making whoopie with Jane Doe while Mrs. Public is out shopping."

"A noble sentiment," Tartaglia said. "But first off, you owe it to me. And second, it doesn't involve kicking in any motel doors. That went out twenty years ago."

He reached into his attaché case and took out a fistful of papers. Diamond thumbed through them. They were financial statements, showing that a working stiff named Sidney Becker was making thirty thou a year, had lots of debts and few assets.

"I can feel for this guy after the wringer that Milly tried to put me through," Diamond said. "It won't be so bad working for him."

"You'll be working for his wife."

"What? How much blood does she want out of the stone?" Diamond dropped the papers on the table. "I'll get the money to pay for your time. Gimme a fair price, and you'll get it."

"Before you get all self-righteous read the articles at the bottom of the stack."

According to the clippings, Sidney Becker was Meyer Lansky's heir. He had enough money to buy Israel and sell it to the Arabs. He was considered a nice guy by mob standards—police only suspected him of a dozen killings on the climb to the top. Justice Department officials said he was worth over a hundred million dollars.

"I don't work for mobsters or their molls," Diamond said.

"I wouldn't work for her either, if she was just another mobster's bimbo," Tartaglia said. "A few years ago, Mrs. Becker had some sort of cancer. I never got exact details. She made peace with herself. She changed and stayed that way even after it went into remission. The money that used to go for clothes and fancy parties she's donating to charities. Everybody from the Red Cross to the Homeless Animal Society has benefited. Sid Becker isn't happy about it. I think it sparked their breakup."

"Okay, so she's not a typical moll," Diamond said, sipping his coffee.

"I'll tell you something honestly," Tartaglia began.

"Can a lawyer do that? Don't it violate your code of ethics?"

"Very funny. You're not the first P.I. I hired."

"What did the other guy find out?"

"Other guys. One called and said he was joining a monastery. Another decided he was moving to Alaska. That day. A third decided the Foreign Legion had great job opportunities. Of course, if you're scared, too, I—"

"Red Diamond ain't scared of nobody."

"Fine. I need someone with determination, initiative, and courage."

"You got him."

"Red, I don't like getting stonewalled my first time out of the box. It's very important to me to do well on this case. I need you to document his income, to prove how much he's really worth."

The lawyer took a file folder out of his case and handed it to Diamond. "I've got to make an appearance. My card's in the folder. Oh, one last thing. Nobody was able to find out where Becker is living."

Becker, sixty, born and raised in New York, had lived a quiet domestic life with the former Anna Mann for thirty-five years. Then he had started his own sexual revolution. If he'd been making notches on his bedpost he would've whittled it down to a matchstick.

He was putting together a musical-comedy movie about a female rock-and-roll band that set off on the road to find America and wound up performing on the stages and in the bedrooms of every city in the country. Casting had taken him two years, and he wasn't done yet.

A society-column photo of Becker showed a bay-windowed satyr with thinning white hair and a sneery smile.

Diamond closed the file and went to his hotel. He was bedding down at the Thompson, a once-second-rate hotel that was now happy to have guests who stayed more than an hour. It had artsy stonework out front, and stone-hard beds inside.

He was thinking of moving back east. The divorce hearing he'd been ordered to gave him a chance to scout around. This Milly dame supposedly had divorced him, but she wasn't getting any alimony, and she wanted to get ahold of his family jewels. If only she knew.

The private-eye business in Los Angeles hadn't been so hot. Red didn't take the run-of-the-mill trade. There had to be a sign that the job could lead to Rocco or Fifi befor3 he'd put on his gumshoes.

He thought about giving Hammer a call. But he knew that would mean a night cruising the bars, with Hammer calling strangers "Commie bastard" and picking fights. And Diamond would have to bail him out.

He didn't have time to bend elbows with the other New York eyes—Reg De Puyster, Pete Chambers, John Bent, Toussaint Moore, Matt Scudder, Miles Jacoby, Dan Fortune, Jack LeVine, Johnny Milano, Ed Noon.

If he went drinking with one, he'd have to do it with all. There'd be hurt feelings if they knew he was in town and didn't hoist a few with them.

He re-reviewed the file. He was looking forward to

13

taking on Becker. "Judge a man by his enemies, not his friends," Marlowe had said one evening as they tailed a rum-runner on his way to the gambling ship off Bay City.

Becker would make a good enemy. He was mobbed up the wazoo. Which meant he had to have connections with Rocco Rico. You couldn't get that high with the wise guys without having dealings with Rocco.

Chapter Two

Rocco Rico had more blood on his hands than a stock-yard slaughterer. Guys, gals, kids, puppies, and kittens, anything that got in Rocco's way, he crushed. Sometimes he did it just for fun, to keep a hand in.

I caught up with him in New York, but things didn't go as I planned. A trio of his hoods got the drop on me, and we wound up at the top of the Empire State Building.

Twenty twittering tourists stood frozen as the wind whistled a funeral march for me. There was no way for them to get to help without risking their own necks.

Rocco's beetle brows crawled, his thick lips pulled back in a bad imitation of a smile as his goons held me at the railing.

"You're gonna make a lasting impression on this town," Rocco cracked, and his goons broke up like he was Buster Keaton and Charlie Chaplin rolled into one.

"You're about as funny as a flat tire in the middle of the Mojave. With no spare," I said.

A three-hundred-pound gorilla with custom brass knuckles on sausage-thick fingers played knock-knock on my kidneys. He thought my pain was as big a barrel of yuks as Rocco's joke.

15

"Where's Fifi?" I asked through gritted teeth.

"I might as well tell you, shamus, since the only place you're going is down."

Gorilla laughed and slugged me again. I felt a jagged shooting pain that gave new meaning to the word "hurt."

"She's over in Jersey. At my warehouse. When I get done with you, I'm gonna go back and take care of her. Then I turn her over to Momo and the boys."

Momo was the gorilla's name. He snorted like a pig at a trough.

Rocco leaned in close and whispered in my ear. "She's trussed up and ready to give treats. There's no one around for miles. She can scream and scream and scream."

I mumbled back at him.

"What?"

I mumbled again.

He put his ear near my mouth. "What did you say, shamus? And make it good. It's your last words."

"Murphisturngle."

"What?"

"Ahhhhhhhhhhhhhhh!" I screamed in his ear. He fell backwards, knocking into one of his boys. The pug holding me went to help his boss, loosening his grip on my right arm.

I don't ask for much in life, and I guess the Boss upstairs decided to answer my prayers.

I whacked one thug in the throat with a forearm and he started making choking noises that sounded like music to me. Another caught my size eleven where you'd least want to catch it. I guess he's singing now with Ina Ray Hutton's all-girl orchestra.

"Get him, get him, Momo!" Rocco shrieked, stepping out of the fray like the chicken he was.

I snapped a few jabs at Momo. He paid as much attention to the blows as I do to sand flies. I knew if he connected

16

with me, even using the hand without the knucks, I would remember it.

He swung wildly. I dodged and jabbed, hooked and crossed like Benny Leonard in his prime. But Momo kept backing me up. Tourists watched as he lumbered after me. A good Samaritan tried to stop Momo. He ran into a back-hand and went beddy-bye.

We circled the observation deck three times, until the tour guides started acting like we were part of the show. Then Momo closed in. I used a nickel-a-view telescope for cover. You can't hide a six-foot shamus behind a metal stanchion.

As Momo reached for me, I spun the telescope head on its yoke, kissing his jaw with a hard metal uppercut that made him see stars. Without my putting a coin in the slot.

As he staggered back, I hit him with everything I had, and some stuff I had to borrow. My fists were sore, but the man-mountain hit the deck with a thud they could hear out in Montauk.

I raced to where I'd last seen Rocco. He was gone. I knew where he was headed. If I didn't get there first, the doll that's got my heart in her pocket was in a heap of trouble.

Diamond came out of his daydream and called Tartaglia's office. The friendly secretary told him to hold.

"Your secretary sounds cute," Diamond said when Tartaglia got on the line.

"She'll be flattered. It's my mother. She's filling in until I can afford someone else. I'm the only lawyer I know who gets homemade chicken soup and pasta for lunch."

"How's the legal-eagle biz?" Diamond asked.

"Another continuance. The plaintiff's attorney hasn't gotten paid yet."

"Waiting for Mr. Green, Your Honor."

17

"Who else? So, are you ready to tackle Becker?"

"Just wind me up and point me in the right direction." As Diamond spoke, he tossed a roll of nickels in the air, caught it, and pocketed it.

Max Latin had taught him the trick. Brass knucks made the cops look at a guy funny, but a roll of coins could be carried without arousing suspicion. And with a fist wrapped around it, the nickels could make change for the toughest palooka. Of course Red had his trusty .38, but sometimes—like when he was breaking and entering—he didn't carry it. He could talk his way out of a burglary beef most of the time, but cops, especially New York cops, got hinky when a piece was involved.

"I'd like to meet Becker's wife. See if she can fill in any background on him."

"I'm sure she'll be willing. She's at their house on the North Shore. We'll take a ride out there tonight."

"Have you eaten?"

"No."

"Why don't we go to Lindy's and then hit the road?"

"Red, Lindy's has been closed for years. Why don't we go to Slotnick's? I'll check with Anna, but I'm sure she'll see us. Meet you in an hour?"

The meal sat nicely in his gut as Diamond drove them out to Lloyd Harbor. Tartaglia was a good listener, and he regaled him with tales of shootouts with bootleggers, smashing white-slavery rings, and rescuing innocents from opium dens.

"It sounds so ancient, but you can't be more than forty-five," Tartaglia said.

"I'm timeless."

The lawyer grunted. He spoke about his life, coming out of law school set to clean up the streets, then getting sick of the politics and bureaucracy of the D.A.'s office, the struggles of starting a practice.

18

"Why do you keep staring at the rear-view mirror?" the young attorney asked. "Am I boring you?"

"I haven't missed a word. But I think we're being followed."

"Which one?" Tartaglia asked, peering out the back window.

"The yellow Datsun, about six car lengths back, in the number two lane."

"I see him. How do you know he's tailing us?"

Annoyed, Diamond said, "You got to trust your instincts. Lots of times that's all that separates you from a few grams of hot lead and an early grave."

"But how do you know?"

Diamond tapped his forehead. "It's up here."

"Can you give me anything more specific?"

"What's with the cross-examination?"

"Occupational hazard. I sincerely would like to learn how you know," Tartaglia said in a conciliatory tone.

"Well, you check your rear mirror a bunch and look for the same car. Speed up, slow down, and see what happens. This yahoo followed every move I've made."

They rode in silence for a few moments as Diamond thought back to the time the Continental Op had first shown him the art of spotting and losing a tail on the winding, hilly streets of San Francisco. Here there was no curvy Lombard Street to ditch an unwanted companion on.

"Who do you think it is?" Tartaglia asked, convinced after Diamond exited the Long Island Expressway and then got back on. The Datsun had copied him exactly.

"Who knows? I got more enemies than Remington has bullets. I'll shake him."

He stomped the gas and the G-force pushed them back against the seat. If there was one thing Red could do better than any other dick, it was drive. He swerved in and out of lanes, down the shoulder, off an exit ramp and back on. He slowed to forty miles an hour, then leaned on the accelerator, scooting into a break in traffic that quickly closed behind him.

"We lost him," Diamond said, allowing himself a smoke. "I guess Rocco's having trouble getting good help nowadays."

"Fill me in on this Rocco character."

"He's an evil mastermind, as rotten as egg salad left out in the sun for a week. If there's a quick, dirty buck to be made, Rocco's behind it. Fu Manchu, Moriarty, they were nothing but Rocco's flunkies."

"I see."

"I've almost nailed him a million times, but he keeps slipping away. But once I get Fifi, I can set a trap for him. Then Fifi and me can tie the knot."

"Tell me about her."

"She's the kind of doll men kill for."

"How charming."

"Her baby blues make an armadillo get mushy inside. Her figure takes your breath away. You feel dry in the mouth, weak in the knees, all tongue-tied, just being near her."

"I felt the same way when I had the flu."

Diamond didn't hear him as he thought about his Fifi.

I used the tommy gun I got off the first guard to chill a half-dozen of his buddies. Then I was inside the warehouse, my ears ringing from the slugs I'd thrown.

"Fifi! Fifi!" I yelled, not caring about giving away my position.

"Over here, peeper," Rocco snarled.

Fifi was shackled to the wall, her dress hiked up, baring gams that would make Betty Grable green with envy. She had a gag in her mouth and she struggled to speak.

Underneath her perfectly sculpted chin, Rocco held a ten-inch shiv.

*"Drop the heater or the broad gets a close shave," Rocco
sneered.*

*If I gave up the gun, the weasel would probably kill us
both, and continue to plunder the world. If I didn't, he'd slit
her throat while I watched. There didn't seem to be much
choice.*

*The Thompson made an angry clang as it hit the con-
crete floor.*

*Rocco ripped the gag from Fifi's mouth. She gasped for
air, then said, "Oh, Red. I'm sorry I got you into this jam."*

"It's okay, cupcake, we been in tighter spots."

*"Can the hearts and flowers, dick. It's curtains for
you."*

"This is the exit," Moses said, and Diamond took them
off the expressway and headed north on New York Avenue, past Huntington, and into Lloyd Harbor.

Diamond saw fewer and fewer houses. Not that they
weren't there, just that they were set back from the road,
out of view behind immaculately trimmed hedges and
oaks, pines, or sycamores.

"Make a left here," Tartaglia said. "Take the next private road you see on the right."

He drove up the dirt road and they came to a heavy
wrought-iron gate. A wiry old man with a bulge under his
blazer stepped out of a red-and-white sentry booth.

"May I help you?" The guy looked like he came from
the wrong side of the subway tracks, but his voice was
Buckingham Palace all the way.

"It's Moses Tartaglia and a guest. Ms. Becker is ex-
pecting us."

"Very good," the guard said, and went back into his
booth. He pressed a button and the gate hummed open.

As Diamond slowly crunched the car down the gravel,
Tartaglia warned him, "Be on your best behavior. The

word on the street is that Anna always was the brains of the household."

Diamond could understand why as he sat in the front parlor of the eighteen-room mansion. Anna was a petite, middle-aged woman who had never been a beauty, but she radiated a cool presence that made you want her to like you.

Her intense brown eyes locked on a visitor like radar homing in on a U-boat. Her depth charges came in a quiet voice that you had to strain to hear.

"My husband started out running numbers for Mike the Mick over in Hell's Kitchen. When Mike became complacent, we agreed that Sid knew the most about the business. I approached Mrs. Ruggiero, who I knew from the market. She broached the subject with her husband. Mr. Ruggiero had also been disappointed with Mike's work. Right around that time Mike met with an unfortunate accident, and Sid took over. Would you care for some tea?"

"No thanks, but a cup of java would do nicely."

"I'll go tell the cook. Moses?"

"Coffee for me, too, if you don't mind?"

"Not at all. It's so pleasant to have company. I don't get out as much as I used to."

After she was gone from the room, Diamond said, "That's some classy lady. Reminds me of the Duchess of Shafter. Did I ever tell you—"

"Later, Red. Let me fill in some details the classy lady neglected to mention. Mr. Ruggiero was 'Vinnie the Ax' Ruggiero. Mike was found in the Jersey swamps. He had been garroted, shot six times, and had his fingers and tongue cut off."

"Must've cut down on his clarinet playing," Diamond said. "How do you know so much?"

"I was with the O.C. unit in the D.A.'s office. That's how I first met Mrs. Becker. Anyway, we heard from snitches that Mrs. B here told Mrs. R that Mike was skimming."

"I guess being a tattletale paid off," Diamond said, gazing around the amphitheater-sized room.

"For her, yes. And she decorated it herself."

When Mrs. Becker came back in the room, Diamond mentioned how nice the furnishings looked. After a proud speech about finding the Art Deco bric-a-brac in quaint out-of-the-way places, Anna got back to the story of their fortune.

She made the couple sound like classic ma and pa business people, working long hours, delegating as little as possible to subordinates, always making sure the customers got the proper service.

Their business was bookmaking, floating crap and card games, insurance fraud, loan-sharking, and occasional extortion. Anna Becker spoke softly and knowledgeably about layoff payments, house odds, bust-out scams, leg-breaking, and arson.

"Would you like cookies, Mr. Diamond?" Anna asked when she was done with her story.

"No thanks. What I don't understand, you seem to know quite a bit about your husband's assets. Can't you put your finger on them?"

"Sidney is not clever, but he is cautious. With the help of his accountants and a tax lawyer, he has managed to conceal his assets admirably."

While Anna sipped tea from her china cup, Tartaglia explained, "Mr. Becker controls or has interest in over fifty corporations. His own finances are tangled up with dummy trusts and foundations, all done through offshore banks. I've tried piercing the corporate veil, but I haven't been able to get any hard and fast figures on his personal assets."

Anna cleared her throat, signaling she was ready to

23

pick up the conversation. "I already have more than enough money to live comfortably for the rest of my life. But there is an orphan's group that needs a new facility in Hicksville. Moses is arranging the paperwork for me."

Tartaglia nodded.

"My other reason is less altruistic. Every time I hear about Sidney club-hopping with a slut starlet, I want to rip his heart out and toast it in the fireplace," Mrs. Becker said. "The next best thing is taking away his money. I doubt many of his tramp girlfriends would find him attractive if they had to ride the bus together, and not a stretch limousine. Can you help me, Mr. Diamond?"

"Did your husband ever have any business with a weasel named Rocco Rico?"

"I met few of my husband's associates. They were rather provincial Sicilians, who believed a wife should produce babies and delicious pasta. I had no desire to be a mother, and I burn toast."

"But you probably could put more bread on the table than most women. Or men."

She smiled and patted Diamond's arm. "Thank you. I do recall my husband dealing with someone named Rocco a long time ago. It involved a stolen car that Sidney wanted to buy. I convinced him we were better off letting the Cadillac go to a chop shop for parts. Far more profitable."

"Hot cars. Sure, Rocco's been involved in that racket. It must be the same one."

"Who is this Rocco?" Anna asked.

"We really must be going," Tartaglia said. He hurried them out before Diamond could launch into his Rocco Rico soliloquy.

24

Chapter Three

The P.I. dropped Tartaglia at his Yonkers apartment and headed south into the city. It was time for the dirtiest part of investigative work.

Snitches, stoolies, rats, stool pigeons, squealers, informants, informers, Judases, finks.

"The best detectives couldn't find their peckers in the morning without an informant," Carmody had told him as they sat in the stationhouse on West Thirty-fifth Street. Carmody should know; he was one of the sharpest dicks the P.D. had, and the first to catch on to Rocco Rico.

Carmody had gotten an inspector's funeral. Five thousand cops showed up to pay their respects after Rocco's boys caught him alone down by the docks.

Carmody had more felony arrests to his credit than any other copper. Which meant the best informants. Cops didn't pay snitches much. Talking came after a good collar, when a dirt bag decides to give up his brother, father, mother, best friend, to stay out of the Big House.

Diamond had been out of New York for a while. He was sure the stoolies he remembered were dried up or dead. Their life expectancy was shorter than a nearsighted steeplejack's.

There was Jimmy the shoeshine boy, who Race Williams and Diamond had used when they first went after the Flame; Mel Motormouth, the mechanic who fixed cars and parking tickets; Pimples, the mug with the bad skin and the great memory; Ratso, who eavesdropped on the underworld as he crawled around the sewers; Porky, the four-hundred-pounder who had to sell information to support his enormous appetite.

Diamond cruised the old haunts. He started in Chinatown, where he got a meal and blank looks in response to his questions about Wing Wong, the snitch with gold teeth and a brass hand. Charlie Chan had introduced him to Diamond, but both Chan and Wong were staying out of sight.

The P.I. devoured a couple of pork buns and prowled the narrow streets. The smells of fish and rotting fruit were everywhere, with occasional doses of frying food. He was shoulder-to-shoulder with sightseers, gang punks from Hong Kong, and ancients with Confucian serenity.

He crossed Canal Street into Little Italy, looking for Giuseppe the Snake in the cappuccino joints. An old man snapped his thumbnail against his teeth in answer to Diamond's question.

In Greenwich Village, Red looked for Beard, the Beat poet who dealt Mary Jane and played out musical clues on his saxophone. All Diamond got was a few sour notes from a kid with a haircut like a Mohawk Indian.

Diamond swung by the docks. Ratso used to hang out in a bar called Nibbles. It must've changed owners. Now the sign above the door said it was TUSH and the gunsels inside reminded Diamond of Arthur Geiger and his boyish pal Carol Lundgren. A scrawny swish in black leather asked Diamond if he wanted to daisy-chain. His explanation of what that meant made Diamond spit out a mouthful of his five-dollar beer.

There was no one he knew at Union Square Park. The place had as much life as the statue of George Washington ever since word spread about Snickers. The snitch had lived by ratting on cat burglars and eating the pigeons he caught in the park. Rocco had found out about Snickers spilling the beans on a million-dollar jewel heist. Two days later, the stool pigeon was found roasting over a spit near the Williamsburg Bridge.

Red was edgy in Times Square. There was something about the "crossroads of the world" that threw him off balance. He had visions of violence, of abandoned cabs, of a woman who said she was Fifi but wasn't.

He asked hotel night clerks, massage parlor barkers, winos, greasy-spoon hash-slingers, managers, and hookers about Mr. Brown, the straight-shooting rackets boss Diamond had helped out. The only info he picked up was that a trip around the world would cost seventy-five bucks.

He had the feeling everybody knew what he was talking about, but they figured him for heat. He didn't have any long green to grease the wheels right, and the street people wouldn't tell the time if there wasn't something in it for them.

He went into a bar on Forty-third Street and ran his patter by the bartender. "You ever hear of a honcho named Brown? Thaddeus Brown, big numbers boss."

"I don't know nothing about numbers."

"How about Sidney Becker?"

"Don't mean nothing to me."

Diamond got a brew and waited until the head was gone. "Okay, how about Rocco Rico?"

The barkeep shook his head.

"Rocco's the rat bastard behind all the rackets. You must've heard of him," Diamond said in exasperation. "He was the one kidnapping the girls out of movie theaters to sell them into white slavery in Mongolia. He had his headquarters up in the torch of the Statue of Liberty, only no one knew it until I found the spy-ship base there."

27

"I don't have time for ding-a-lings," the bartender said as he walked away to serve another customer.

He had given Diamond a clue. He must be being watched, the P.I. thought, but still he had helped out. Diamond dropped a five on the bar.

He walked to the phone booth in the back of the bar and checked the white pages. There were three entries under Thaddeus Brown. No answer at the first.

The second was a geezer who bent Diamond's ear about how his rheumatism was worse since they dropped the A-bomb. At the third, which was under the heading Thaddeus Brown Enterprises, a molasses-voiced woman answered.

"I'm looking for Thaddeus Brown, who handles the number action north of Thirty-fourth Street," Diamond said.

"Let me switch you to the executive offices," she said coolly.

Diamond had to go through two more secretaries.

"Our founder was reputed to be involved with wagering, though no charges were ever proven," said a woman who identified herself as vice-president in charge of corporate affairs.

"Does he have a build like a fireplug, a gravelly voice, never smiles, and nuts about the color brown?"

"Who did you say you were?" she asked.

"If that's him, tell him Diamond's on the line."

"If you wish to make an appointment, perhaps he can arrange to speak to you. Though I doubt if you have the right person."

"When's he free?"

"Let me switch you to his secretary."

Told the next available moment Brown could meet with him was three months away, Diamond hung up in disgust.

He called back ten minutes later.

"This is Hargrove. IRS. Audit bureau. Get me Brown."

"Let me switch you to accounting," the receptionist said. "You can—"

"I can hit you and your boss and anyone who's ever walked into your office with a subpoena or a jeopardy assessment. What is your name?"

"Hold on please," she said docilely.

Diamond was transferred to Brown's secretary, who was a little harder to bulldoze. He finally convinced her he was calling about Brown's personal taxes, something he might not want his company's accounting department to know about.

"What do you want?" a man's voice growled at Diamond.

"Those sweet and gentle tones can only belong to the ace of spades," Diamond said.

"Who is this?"

"Red Diamond, your favorite white private eye."

"What's with this IRS crap? You got my people running around burning records."

"If you got a pure heart, you need not worry. Your staff wouldn't put me through to you. What scam are you up to anyway? You got more buffers than the head of General Motors."

"I've gone legit."

"Bullshit. Why's everyone burning paper then?"

"Hell, even the President cheats the IRS. It's as American as screwing the underdog. It's been a long time. I hear that you've been doing good work in Los Angeles. And that stint in Las Vegas."

"You got good ears."

"Word travels quick."

"If you know where to go. That's what I'm calling about. I was going to ask for information, but . . ." Diamond hesitated.

"Don't be shy."

"Well, now that you're a respected member of the community, do you still have contacts?"

"I need them more than ever. Who makes sure I get hijacked truckloads of stereos for my stores, or the inspectors don't get greedy about their payoffs, or I get the bootleg videos I ordered?"

"Sounds like you're a real straight arrow."

"It's much easier to rake it in when you go corporate. The world of cops and robbers ain't the same as it used to be, brother. You're part of a dying breed. I was too, until I went straight."

"Your rehabilitation is an inspiration. Anyway, I want to find out about Sidney Becker."

"I know the name. He's a conniver. I hear he's got more Swiss bank accounts than all the dope dealers in Colombia."

"I want to find out where he hangs his hat."

"I'll put my ears out."

When the elevator door opened on his floor, he stood to one side and waited. It was better to be on your toes than wearing a toe tag. He poked his head out and peered down the corridor to his room. Someone was standing outside the door.

Diamond pushed the DOOR CLOSE button and rode the elevator up one floor, walked to the fire stairs, and then padded down to his floor.

He peered out through the small window set in the heavy metal door.

The ambusher wasn't very sharp, standing outside Diamond's door, pacing back and forth like a first-time papa in a maternity ward. He was young, around twenty, and clean-cut. He looked more like a college football star than a strongarm, dressed in a knit shirt, slacks, and jogging sneakers. He was the type you'd expect to see selling raffle tickets or fetching the beer barrel for a blast at the dorm.

30

Just the kind of hard-to-spot talent Rocco would use. He was diabolically clever.

Red got out his rod, took a deep breath, and rumbled into the hall like the Chattanooga Choo-Choo with a full head of steam.

Diamond slammed Mr. Clean-cut against the wall and burrowed the gun in his ear.

"One sound outta you and I puncture your eardrum with a .38 slug," Diamond snarled.

Mr. Clean-cut's mouth dropped open. Diamond got out his keys and opened the door to his room. The P.I. shoved him hard and he fell to the floor. Diamond stepped in and locked the door.

Red stood over him, pointing the .38 at a spot between Mr. Cleancut's brows. He cocked the hammer.

"All right, you two-bit gunsel, what've you got to say for yourself?"

"Hi, Dad."

Chapter Four

Diamond froze and locked eyes with the young man. The face the P.I. saw was innocent, compelling, and did bear a slight resemblance to his own. It was a face Diamond knew, and the painful déjà vu washed over him like the Pacific over Burt Lancaster in *From Here to Eternity*.

"Urgggh," he said, dropping the gun and clutching his head as a migraine as bad as Rocco exploded in his cranium.

"Dad, Dad, is anything the matter?" the young innocent asked sincerely. "Can I get up now?"

"Arrrrghh," Diamond said, trying to squeeze out the pain.

The young man got up and helped Diamond to the bed. As Diamond collapsed he cautiously retrieved the gun and set it down on the dresser.

"Who . . . who are you?" Diamond gasped.

"Sean. Your son. Don't you remember?"

"You must have the wrong room, sonny."

The young man had an eager air about him, as if he hadn't yet run into a problem he couldn't solve. Even looking down the wrong end of a gun hadn't fazed him. It wasn't from toughness so much as Pollyannaish optimism.

"Don't you remember me?" the kid was asking.

"Did that dame Milly send you? Is this part of the scam?"

"She doesn't know I'm here."

"Who sent you? How'd you find me? Where are my cigarettes?"

"You smoke?"

"What's wrong with smoking? It goes with the territory."

"Haven't you read the Surgeon General's report?"

"What the hell are you talking about?" Diamond asked, snatching a pack from the night table, tearing it open, and lighting the cigarette as he put it in his mouth.

"I need your help," Sean said.

"How?"

"Melonie. She ran away."

The throbbing resumed as he said, "Who's Melonie?"

"My sister. Your daughter. You really don't remember?"

"I don't know what bunco act you're working, but Red Diamond won't fall for it."

"Dad, please. It's been hard since you left. Mom went a little crazy. She . . . she saw a lot of men. It really hurt Melonie. Even though Melonie was wild herself, she didn't like seeing it in Mom. Melonie . . ."

The young man stopped talking to fight back the tears.

"All right, all right, turn off the showers. What do you want from me anyway?"

"She disappeared eighty-four days ago. She used to disappear with boyfriends, but this is different. She got in with a fast crowd. I tried stopping her."

"Kid, I'm on a case. When I get finished, I'll put a day or so into it and see what I turn up. No charge."

"It can't wait. I tried. I really did. I still kept a 3.9 cum at Stony Brook, but I had to drop the soccer team. You'd be

33

proud of me, Dad. But I'm not as good an investigator as you are. I lost track of her. Will you help me? Please."

"As soon as I polish off this other case."

"What if she's dead? Or worse."

"There ain't too much worse than being dead. Unless you've spent a week in Philadelphia."

Sean didn't respond.

"Anyway, if she's dead it don't matter. She's been gone that long, she's probably found a safe spot. Now, I'm dead on my feet. If I don't get some shut-eye, I won't be worth nothing to nobody. So how about you go back to college and I hit the hay."

"But you will help me?"

"Sure."

"That's great. Thanks, Dad."

"Do me a favor?"

"Anything."

"Stop calling me Dad. It makes me feel like I dropped out of a Norman Rockwell cover."

"What should I call you? Sy?"

Diamond felt a twinge of a headache. "No. Call me Red. Or Mr. Diamond. Or Red Diamond. Or hey you."

"Okay. Red," Sean said.

He took a few steps toward the door. "Would you really have shot me?"

"Only if you blinked."

Diamond had protected Lana Turner from Johnny Stompanato. She was about to reward the P.I. for his derring-do by removing her sweater, when the phone rang, waking him from his dream. He glared at his watch. It was 8 A.M.

"Uhhhh," he grumbled into the phone.

"The early bird catches the Dow Jones morning report," Brown said cheerfully.

"Do you know what time it is?"

"In New York, or in my Hong Kong office, or my Swiss office? It's never too early. I've been at my desk for an hour already. You're never gonna make it if you don't get out of bed."

Diamond stretched. "What's up?"

"Becker's place. Got a piece of paper?"

Diamond did, and Brown read him an address on Fifty-second near the East River.

"He sublets a two-bedroom, with a view of the harbor. Set up a cozy little crib." Brown said. "You watch yourself."

"Don't worry. I'm a big boy."

"So's his bodyguard. A bone-crusher named Bruno. He was on Death Row for a while, until the other inmates complained he was a bad influence. He got sprung on appeal."

"Sounds real appealing. Thanks for the info."

"You be careful. There ain't many white folks I give a damn about."

Diamond rolled out of bed and over to the radio built into the wall. The sounds of Peter Piper and the Pickled Peppers singing the joys of dual carb exhausts blasted out at him. He quickly spun the dial to a big-band station.

He did calisthenics, push-ups, and sit-ups to a slew of Benny Goodman tunes. Diamond was in the shower as Harry James trumpeted his way through "You Made Me Love You."

He found himself tapping his toes to memories of "Sing, Sing, Sing" as he primed himself for the day with a deluxe meal at the greasy spoon next to the hotel.

Tartaglia was in when he called. He was amazed when Diamond said he'd already tracked Becker down.

"I thought I had made a mistake with you," the lawyer said. "You're kind of different. But you get results. What are you going to do?"

"Thanks for the vote of confidence," Diamond said sarcastically. "I'll share something I picked up from Kearny at DKA in Frisco."

"Run that by me again."

"DKA is Kearny's agency. I helped them out once, wound up trapped on Alcatraz with a mob of kill-crazy cons and trigger-happy screws behind me and a pack of bloodthirsty sharks in front of me. Rocco was behind the trap, and—"

"I hate to cut the story short, but I've got a plea-bargaining conference in fifteen minutes."

"I'll tell you later. Anyway, Kearny always said with John Q. Public you can check papers, do a house-to-house canvass, follow the P.I. manual from A to Z. But hard cases don't leave tidbits in the public record, and the neighbors don't gossip about jokers that can blow up their car."

"What are you saying?"

"To get anywhere with Becker, I'm gonna have to take the bull by the horns."

The ropes bit into my hands like hemp piranhas. Rocco stood over me, enjoying my helplessness.

The hook from a heavy chain was looped through the rope. I was hanging hands above my head, feet nearly touching the bubbling chemicals. The pungent stench of acid burned my nostrils.

"We do plating and smelting here," Rocco said gleefully. "Now we're going to see what it takes to melt a diamond."

Fifi was strapped to a chair at the far side of the room. Her skimpy dress hung off one shoulder, and looked like it would fall with a puff of air. Her terrific twosome were as set on freedom as a band of Maquis.

"If she marries me, shamus, I make it quick and easy

for you. Otherwise, we make it last for days, lower you in, inch by inch. Now, tell her to marry me!"

"Go suck a muffler, louse."

He signaled and a henchman in the control booth of the crane hit a switch. The hook lowered, leaving my tootsies an inch above the tank.

"What do you say?" Rocco cackled.

"Your mother wears combat boots. Kraut combat boots. She's got feet the size of ferryboats."

He clenched his teeth and signaled again.

I was just over the surface of the fatal fluid. I could feel the bubbles breaking against my shoes. There was the smell of burning leather.

"I'll marry you, I'll marry you, Rocco," my doll shrilled.

"Don't do it, cupcake. You'll be miserable."

"I can't bear to see you suffer, Red darling," she said.

"Ain't that wonderful," Rocco sneered. "He's gotta say it. And mean it."

"These ropes are tight on my hands, Rocco," she pleaded. "Could you loosen them. This isn't a nice way to start our honeymoon."

He smirked at me and walked to her. She had wiggled a bit, giving him quite a view of her gorgeous globes. He took his time fiddling with her ropes.

I began to swing back and forth. The thug working the crane was watching Rocco fumble with my sweet patootie.

She kept him busy, wriggling and giggling. It boiled my blood, the sacrifice she had to make, chumming up to that horrible heel.

I got momentum and swung off the hook just as he turned. I charged him like a rhino, head down, growling and grunting and not worrying about the Mauser in Rocco's hand sending rounds over my head.

He wasn't a bad shot, but he was scared. I was coming

at him like there was no tomorrow. 'Cause if one of his slugs connected, for me there wouldn't be.

I butted him and he dropped the heater. I lunged for the bum, my hands still bound. The soles of my shoes had been melted away. It made me move like Bronko Nagurski had crushed me with a flying tackle.

Rocco sidestepped and we struggled. Fifi tried to kick him. His henchman winged shots down at us from the booth. He couldn't draw a bead on me without risking hitting Rocco.

Then a shot went wild. The ricochet hit Fifi. I heard her scream and stopped pounding Rocco's head against the concrete. He scooted off like a rat on the Lusitania with his flunky not far behind.

I hoisted Fifi in my arms, no easy feat with the rope still holding my hands together. I put her across my shoulder like a delectable sack of laundry and ran to the car. She was bleeding pretty bad. If I didn't get her to a hospital pronto, I'd be visiting her at Peaceful Meadows Cemetery.

The hospital was only ten minutes away. I knew I could make it.

I hadn't counted on Rocco's roadblock.

Red took the FDR Drive to Becker's luxury building. It was a red-brick high-rise, recently sandblasted, with freshly painted windows, terraces, and well-kept potted plants next to plush furniture in the lobby.

The doorman was dressed like the palace guard to a South American dictator, an aging soldier prepared to give his life to repulse invaders.

"Hey, how's it going?" Diamond asked, thrusting out his hand and keeping a bumpkin expression on his face.

The doorman looked at him imperiously. "Can I help you?"

"I sure hope so. My name's Fred. Fred Farmer. I'm

just in from Ohio, see, and I got ol' Sidney's address from the alumni office. I'd like to surprise him."

"I'm sure he'd be surprised. Unfortunately, he's not in at the moment."

"Too bad, too bad. I reckon in a fancy building like this, you wouldn't want a fella hanging around in the halls waiting for his buddy."

"That's correct."

Diamond offered a cigarette to the doorman. He accepted, but kept a baleful eye on the P.I. as Diamond lit up.

"Good ol' Sidney. Always a fun guy. I was hoping he could let me get a peek at his little black book. He had more action than he knew what to do with, if you know what I mean . . ."

Diamond left the sentence dangling, but the doorman refused to pick it up.

"What's your name?" Diamond asked.

"Frank."

"What a coincidence. I'm Fred and you're Frank. Well, Frank, do you have any idea where I could find my buddy?"

"No."

"How about when he's coming back?"

"No."

"Where he works?"

"No."

Diamond fished a ten-spot out of his billfold. "Would this help you recollect better?"

"No."

"I see. Well, I'd really like to stay here all day and chew the fat, but I got to be moseying on."

"I'll tell Mr. Becker you were by."

"Don't bother. Like I said, I'd like to make it a surprise."

Diamond walked around the block. There was a service entrance at the side of the building, out of view of the doorman.

He waited until a truck came delivering bottled water. He passed just as the delivery man unlocked the security door. The P.I. got a warm thanks for holding the door open. The water bearer didn't see the matchbook cover Diamond wedged in the door so it couldn't close properly.

He rode up to the penthouse and checked the door to Becker's apartment. Other dicks boasted they could pick a lock with a bobby pin and some spit. Red knew that even with his pick set, it would take him at least an hour to get through the three deluxe locks on Becker's reinforced door.

Diamond walked to the window at the end of the short hallway. He looked down twenty stories and saw the tugs plying their trade in the swift-moving river. There was a small ledge outside, wide enough to support a couple of pigeons comfortably. As long as they weren't too pudgy. He opened the window and climbed out.

The wind was stronger than he expected. It tugged at him like a lonely child, begging him to try flying. He tried to squeeze his two-hundred-pound body into the cracks in the brick wall.

He edged down the ledge, each step knocking years off his life expectancy. A gull stood defiantly in front of him, refusing to move. It had a smile on its beak.

"Beat it, beat it," Diamond said, but the wind whipped his words. He couldn't move any part of his body to frighten the cocky bird off.

The gull was as big as a Flying Fortress. When it seemed like he was about to do hand-to-talon combat, it took off, flapping great white wings and guffawing.

Diamond climbed over a wrought iron railing and stepped onto Becker's terrace. The sliding glass door was solid in its tracks. He hefted Becker's hibachi and created work for a glazier. He stepped cautiously across the pale blue shag carpet, which was now covered with glass shards.

Becker's pad was an adolescent's bachelor fantasy, with nude paintings on dark mahogany walls, mammoth cushions scattered everywhere, a wet bar and fireplace in the center of the room. A panel with as many switches as a P-38 cockpit controlled lights, stereo, tape and video decks, room temperature, and the gas flame in the fireplace.

In the bedroom, Diamond found a waterbed, trapeze, and ropes. There were hundreds of books, magazines, and photos. In one or two of the pictures, people were wearing clothes. Becker liked them young, and he wasn't that particular about which gender. With his underworld connections, Becker could get the hardest filth floating around the smut sewers.

Diamond's indignation was doing a high-wire act when he hit a color photo that made his neck hairs stand on end.

It showed a girl in her late teens at a man's feet. The girl wore an outfit made out of enough black leather to make a good-sized watchband. She was thin with pigtails and a world-weary face. She reminded him of Milly. But something . . .

His temples throbbed.

The man in the photo was only visible from the navel down. He was naked. His legs were so hairy it looked like he was wearing black pants. He had flabby thighs and jelly-roll calves. Rocco!

Diamond could recognize that hirsute form anywhere. He pocketed the picture and a few of Becker, where the aging satyr was identifiable, groping teens.

Red prowled the apartment—looking in closets, drawers, and on shelves—but didn't find anything worth snatching until he came to the rolltop desk just outside the bathroom.

Diamond opened it and found Becker's bills. He was thumbing through the stack when he heard a key in the lock.

Chapter Five

Diamond ducked into the bathroom. He peeked through the partially opened door. It was Bruno. Either that, or the Fuller Brush man with a .45 ready in his mitt.

The bodyguard was better than six-foot and nearly as broad across the shoulders. He moved with the languid grace of a lion on the hunt. He had a protruding jaw, a sloping forehead, and a wicked gleam in his dark eyes as he stalked his prey.

It was only a matter of time. Diamond looked around the bathroom. Not very promising. A translucent shower stall, mirrored medicine cabinet, miscellaneous toiletries, and the john itself. There was a hook with clothes hanging on it.

He could hear Bruno prowling closer.

The P.I. silently hung the clothes in the shower. Through the semi-opaque glass it looked like someone hiding in the stall. Diamond held his breath and waited. Time crawled by.

The door of the bathroom slowly eased open. The lights went on. Bruno spotted the form in the shower.

The .45 was deafening in the small room as the bodyguard pumped three shots into the shower. Bruno's arm was half in the door when Diamond slammed it shut, catching the strongarm's hand. Diamond leaned on the door until the .45 hit the tile floor.

A fist punched through the wooden bathroom door and groped like something out of *The Cat and the Canary*. Diamond rapped the knuckles with his roll of coins.

Bruno couldn't get in, but Red couldn't get out, or even bend to pick up the fallen gat. Bruno shook the door and tried reaching through the hole he'd made again.

"Gonna kill you," Bruno growled after a yowl of pain.

"How about you call me a nasty name and let me go."

Bruno redoubled his efforts to tear the door out of its frame.

The P.I. grabbed an aerosol can of deodorant.

"Hey, Bruno," Diamond said. "I wanna show you something."

"What?"

Bruno put his eye to the hole in the door, and Diamond treated him to a cloud of Right Guard.

Bruno screamed and stopped slamming against the door. Diamond let up his pressure, snatched the .45 off the floor, and stepped out into the living room. Bruno was clutching his face.

"Why don't you go wash up," Diamond suggested amiably as Bruno tried to tear his eyes out of their sockets. He barreled into the bathroom and rinsed frantically.

Diamond tucked the .45 under his jacket and strolled out whistling "Rhapsody in Blue." He lit a cigarette and drove back to his hotel.

The tires screeched like a pack of bobby-soxers who'd just missed Frankie at the Paramount stage entrance. I leaned on the gas and we roared down the road.

The Duesenberg speedster meant business. It's too flashy for most jobs, but when I have to put the blitz on, she eats up the road.

43

Fifi was leaking her transmission fluid on my leather seats. The upholstery was replaceable. My doll wasn't.

I was hitting ninety when I saw Rocco's boys, with heaters in their hands and a matched set of DeSotos parked blocking the road.

The lead started flying and spider webs of cracks formed on the windshield. If I reached for my shooting iron, I'd lose control of the wheel, and we'd be scrambled over easy on the high cliffs.

We hit the DeSotos and sent them careening. I was glad them Duesenbergs knew how to make a heavy-duty chassis. We were spinning like a dizzy dervish on a carnival ride.

I pulled out of it and leaned on the gas again. The car groaned. Old Duesie had been wounded by the collision. But she wouldn't let me and Fifi down.

"Ohhhh, Red, what happened?" Fifi moaned.

"You put on a little weight, babe. A few ounces of lead. But you're gonna be okay."

"I know I will. I'm with you."

She leaned over, resting her beautiful blond head on my shoulder. I could smell her Shalimar perfume.

Somewhere along the way her dress had vaporized. Halfway to heaven, my angel had more sex appeal than a Flo Ziegfeld chorus line. She was as pale as the marble of an Italian statue.

"C'mon Duesie, let's get moving," I whispered to the injured car. The speedometer needle climbed over 100.

I looked in the mirror. The DeSotos must've been supercharged. It was time to make like Jesse Owens.

The Duesie began to smoke. I looked at the radiator gauge. It was off the dial, hotter than Jack Teagarden's trombone on a Saturday night at the Hotel Astor.

I waited until we got around a curve and out of sight of the fast-moving goon squad. I braked, jumped out, and carried Fifi into the woods.

I went back to the car and got my spare can of gas. I dribbled the gas in a trail from under the Duesie's big tank to behind a boulder.

The DeSotos squealed up. Six rats with roscoes hopped out and crept to the Duesenberg. They opened fire with chatter guns, turning my favorite car into Swiss cheese.

"All right, check it out," the head hood ordered, and they closed in on their target.

I lit a match and tossed it on the gas trail and ran to Fifi. I was lifting her onto my shoulder when I heard the blast and the screams.

I took off for the hospital in a commandeered DeSoto.

"We'll be at the hospital in a minute, Fifi baby. Hang on."

She didn't answer.

At 120 miles an hour, each curve was a challenge. But I had other curves on my mind. The 38-24-36 curves of my blond bombshell.

We zoomed up to the emergency room entrance.

A skinny hospital cop with a droopy mustache and a cannon strapped to his narrow hips got in my way.

"Parking for emergency vehicles only."

"My girl, she's been shot."

"Only authorized emergency vehicles can park here. If you get a permit from the adminis——"

He didn't know what hit him. I lifted Fifi and we stepped over the glass-jawed geek.

"Quick, get me 50 ccs of plasma," the doc said as soon as he saw her. Nurses took my love bundle and laid her on a gurney. A team in white smocks circled her and began doing the Florence Nightingale number.

"Anything I can do, doc?" I asked when one of the sawbones came up for air.

"No. You made it here just in time. She's gonna be okay."

45

But he and I didn't know the rotten surprise Rocco had in store for us.

Diamond lit another cigarette and looked over the papers spread out on his hotel-room bed.

There was a knock at the door. The .38 was under his pillow. He grabbed Bruno's .45 from off the dresser. "Who's there?"

"It's me, Dad. Sean."

Diamond lowered the gun and opened the door. "Red. Do me a favor and call me Red."

"I'm sorry. I've got so much on my mind."

"We all do, kid. What do you want?"

"You have to help me find Melonie. It's urgent."

"I'm on a case, Sean. One of the rules of the game is never let a client down, never drop one job for another. What would you think of Philip Marlowe if he dumped Moose Malloy soon as General Sternwood came along?"

"Dad, I brought something I want you to see," Sean said, lifting the photo album he carried at his side.

"I ain't got time for a trip down Memory Lane. Especially since it ain't my lane we're going down. I'm working, kid. Come back another time."

"Please, Dad."

"Take a picture of your sister and show it around her hangouts. Don't waste it on me. And if you don't stop calling me Dad, I'm gonna put you across my knee and give you a spanking."

Sean opened the book. "Look, here's you and Mom on your honeymoon at Niagara Falls," he said, pointing to a yellowed black-and-white snapshot. "Here's a picture of you with me and Melonie at Jones Beach."

Diamond averted his eyes like a child who didn't want to see a frog being dissected.

"Here you are when you first got the cab. I remember

that. I sat on your lap and we went for a ride. You let me hold the steering wheel and pretend I was driving."

"Uhhhhhhh," Diamond said, as his head began to throb.

"And here's Melonie at her junior-high prom. You and Mom had a fight over whether her dress was cut too low. Do you remember that?"

The girl in the photo was the same as he'd seen in the picture of Rocco. From junior-high proms to black leather.

"Arrrrrrrrruuuuuuuuugggh," Diamond cried as the pain of a million migraines burst in his head. He fell to the floor clutching his skull.

"Dad! Dad!"

"Urrrrrrrrrrrrrrgggggggooooooooh."

Sean knelt. "I'm sorry. I just wanted to shock you back into reality. My psych textbook said that for traumatic psychosis, it's—"

"What's going on, Sean? Where's Mom?"

"Dad?"

He nodded.

"Simon. Simon Jaffe?" Sean asked.

"Who else would I be?" Jaffe asked, looking around bewildered. "Where am I?"

"It worked," Sean said happily.

"Ohhh," Jaffe groaned as he sat down on the bed. "I wanna catch my breath, then we better get going. You know how your Mother is if we're late for dinner."

"Dad, you and Mom are finalizing a divorce."

"For what? For being late for dinner a few times?"

"You don't remember? Mom got rid of your books. You ran off and began acting out the role of one of the characters you read about. Red Diamond."

"The name rings a bell. Sure, a real tough private eye. By Scott Marks."

"You used the hardboiled tricks of the trade you'd

47

picked up from your reading. You actually helped some people out. A Mr. Brown in Harlem. A Gwen Manfred out in Los Angeles and a millionaire in Las Vegas, Ed Evans. I bet you had others," Sean said curiously.

"Those names are sorta familiar, in a blurry way. The divorce is too," Jaffe said, rubbing his drooping head. He looked up hopefully. "Do you think Milly will forgive me if I brought her a box of Barricini's chocolate and roses?"

"Dad, you've been away two years." He hesitated. "I . . . I think she's got a boyfriend."

Jaffe sagged into the bed. He covered his face with his hands.

"I'm sorry I did this to you," Sean said. "But I need your help. Melonie's missing."

"Maybe she's with that artist in SoHo, the one who makes portraits out of tapioca?" Jaffe asked in a weak voice.

"That was a long time ago. She's been through about thirty lovers since then," Sean said disgustedly. "There was a sculptor who turned out to be married. To two women. A rock-group drummer, who was cut in half by his automatic garage-door opener. And a mechanic who ran off after borrowing her clothing. I lost track.

"Four months ago, she got involved with a guitarist from a rock band. Three months ago, he turned up dead in the Bronx. He was in that *Newsweek* write-up on rockers who burn their candles at both ends. Anyway, she disappeared right after he was buried."

Jaffe was alert. "Have you gone to the police?"

Sean nodded. "She's over eighteen. They say she can do whatever she wants."

"How did the musician die?"

"Drug overdose."

"Do you think Melonie is taking drugs?"

"Dad, don't you remember the time you caught her

48

smoking dope with the three linemen from the football team in the basement? She was naked and they—"

"Enough. She's a good girl. Anyone can make a mistake once."

"Then what about the time she took LSD, and turned up in the locker room while the basketball team—"

"She just likes athletes. There's nothing wrong with that."

"And musicians. Car dealers, artists, traveling salesmen, freelance—"

"Maybe your mother can have a talk with her."

"Mom's got her own problems, Dad. That's why I came to you. Since you're such a great detective, I know we can find her. What should we do?"

"It's nice you care so much about your sister."

"We hate each other, Dad. We always have. But I've been the man in the house. You taught me to take care of my little sister."

Jaffe rubbed his face, shook his head, and paced around the room. Although Jaffe and Diamond shared the same body, their use of the muscles and bones was completely different. Where Diamond bobbed with a confident swagger, Jaffe moved his tired frame like he was carrying the weight of the world on his stooped shoulders.

"I don't know what to do," Jaffe said. He spotted the .45. "Where did this come from?" he asked, picking it up like it was a bubonic-flea-infested rodent.

"It must be yours."

"We better get rid of it. I read that people who have guns are six times more likely to get shot. Or shoot themselves."

"Please, try and think. What would Red Diamond do to find Melonie?"

"Uh, I guess he'd talk to the boyfriend."

"He's dead."

49

"Oh yeah. Then we better go to the police."

"I did that already."

"Right. Uh, maybe we should ask your mother."

Sean sighed.

"I guess that's not right." He sat back on the bed, crushing Becker's papers.

"Oooops, what's this? These papers, they belong to someone named Sidney Becker. How did they get here?"

"I don't know. What about Melonie?"

"I'm thinking, I'm thinking." Jaffe glanced at the bills. "Look at this. Sidney Becker spends four hundred dollars for a meal. And these other bills. Whooo boy!"

It was quiet in the room.

"I got an idea," Jaffe said triumphantly. "Why don't we ride up to Becker and return the papers. I always think better when I'm in the cab."

"The cab's long gone. You abandoned it in Times Square. Mom sold it for scrap."

"Jeez. How am I gonna make a living?" Jaffe said in a panicky tone. "I'll have to get a job with the fleets. I bet Becker can help. It could be a lucky break, his papers turn up in my room like this. How we gonna get this back to him?"

"Mail it."

"No. It looks important. I tried to teach you kids to be courteous. I ever tell you about the time I returned this fare's wallet that he'd left in the cab, and he gave me a fifty-dollar tip?"

"Sure. But there was a thousand dollars in the wallet."

"Still, I had the satisfaction of doing the right thing and getting rewarded for it. We can get rid of this gun and go to Mr. Becker's apartment."

"What about Melonie?"

"We can ask this Mr. Becker. He's rich. He must be smart. Maybe he can give us advice."

50

"I've read his name somewhere."

"Rich people are always getting their names in the papers. He'll be so happy with us bringing this back, he'll want to do something special for us."

"I don't have a good feeling about this."

"You've got to learn to follow the golden rule. Do unto others as you would have others do unto you."

Chapter Six

A grinning Bruno opened the door.

Becker, whose thinning hair stuck up in white tufts, beckoned them in. He was wearing a purple velvet robe that gaped open in the front, exposing a protruding pot belly that had the same frizzy tufts as his head.

"It's so nice of you to return these," Becker said, taking the papers from Jaffe. He looked at Sean. "Such a handsome chap. In good shape. Do you work out?"

"I'm on the boxing, gymnastics, and soccer teams."

"He plays intercollegiate chess, too. And keeps honor grades. I'm real proud of him."

"And well you should be," Becker said. "When you called offering to return my papers, I could hardly believe it. You don't expect that kind of behavior nowadays. Thanks so much. Bruno, see these gentlemen out."

A disappointed Jaffe started to speak, then gave up. He shook Becker's hand and took a few steps toward the door before the lights went out.

He awoke feeling like someone had stomped on the back of his head. Becker and Bruno loomed over him. He was tied to an English Windsor wooden chair.

"All right, wise guy, what's the game?" Becker growled.

"Huh?"

"Frank called from downstairs when he saw you. You're the one that was asking around right before my place got burglarized. Then you come back with the stolen property. What kind of putz do you think I am?"

"I don't know what you're talking about."

Bruno backhanded Jaffe four times. The cabbie's head rocked and rolled even after the blows stopped.

"I've got all kinds of toys," the elderly satyr said. "I think shock therapy with the cattle prod will get you going. Bruno has fun with the cattle prod. Right, Bruno?"

The gorilla grunted his assent.

"Honest, I don't know what you're talking about."

"You don't know about the business cards in your pocket—'Red Diamond, Private Eye'?"

"No. I been out of it for a while. Sean can explain. Where is he?"

Becker chuckled and signaled Bruno, who walked out to the terrace. A heavy rope was looped around the railing. Bruno pulled up on the rope and Sean's legs came into view.

"We're letting the blood rush to his head. Hopefully, you'll talk before we have to cut the rope. I hate to see such a fine young body go splat on the sidewalk."

"Please, believe me. This is a mistake. Let us go. I promise we won't tell the police or anything."

"The police?" Becker laughed. "Bruno, he promises not to tell the police."

Bruno's laugh was a cavernous roar.

"The last time I had a problem, Bruno played with the troublemaker for a week. He was able to toss the body into the river from the terrace. Of course the bastard weighed less. He had lost a lot of blood."

Jaffe blinked as rivulets of sweat ran into his eyes.

"In the Arab countries, they cut off a thief's hands," Becker said. "I think it's appropriate, don't you?"

53

"Please, let my kid go," Jaffe begged. "Whatever happened, he had nothing to do with it."

"How moving, the plea of a helpless father to save his son. Bruno, get me a knife."

Bruno went into the kitchen and reappeared with a long blade. He handed it to Becker.

"Bruno is a gourmet cook. The knives are kept razor-sharp. You could shave with it." Becker touched the blade to Jaffe's chin and a droplet of blood appeared.

Jaffe closed his eyes.

"Open your eyes. Bruno's going to cut your boy loose."

"Thank you, thank you, Mr. Becker," Jaffe said.

The strongarm walked to the terrace, lifted the rope, and began to cut.

"Nooooooo!" Jaffe cried.

"Who hired you! Why did you take my bills?" Becker demanded.

"I don't know. I mean I didn't."

Bruno continued to cut.

"Please stop."

"Who hired you?"

"I don't know."

Bruno kept cutting.

"Sean had nothing to do with it. He knows nothing about anything. He's just a kid."

Jaffe could see the rope beginning to fray. "Please, I'll do anything. I beg you, let him go."

"You'll do anything anyway. Besides, if Bruno doesn't have his fun, he gets cranky."

Bruno locked eyes with Jaffe as he drew the blade across the rope one last time. The hemp parted and the section attached to the young man's legs flew away.

Jaffe passed out.

He awoke to Becker slapping his face.

"You missed seeing the kid hit the pavement. Maybe we can go down and take a look," Becker said.

"Shove it, flamethrower breath. You don't scare me." The words came from the same voicebox as Jaffe's, but they were staccato, without hesitation.

Becker noticed. "Who are you?"

"The boogie-woogie bugle boy."

"Bruno, come here."

"You're a two-bit punk, Becker. If I wasn't tied up, I'd teach you and King Kong a lesson."

"So now I'm supposed to let you loose? So you can fight it out? It doesn't work that way."

"Yellow, huh?"

"Call me whatever you want. I'm not the one strapped to a chair, about to lose his left hand."

The gorilla lifted Diamond's hand and waved the knife with a flourish.

"Leave my Dad alone," Sean said from the terrace.

"Holy shit!" Bruno said.

Diamond kicked Bruno in the shins. Becker ran for a gun. Diamond got up and swung the chair behind him like a four-legged wooden tail. He caught Becker's soft belly, and the satyr went down with an oooof. Diamond kicked him in the head and watched his eyes roll up.

Bruno recovered, raised the knife, and charged Sean, who stood on the terrace with both feet still tied together. Diamond hobbled after the strongarm as quickly as he could.

"Hey, musclehead, how'd you like the deodorant eye-wash?"

Bruno turned and lunged at Diamond, who spun at the last minute. The long knife embedded itself in the wooden chair. Diamond twisted and turned, poking at Bruno with the chair legs.

Sean untied himself and raced in. He assumed a Marquis of Queensberry boxing pose. Bruno turned his attention from Diamond and attacked Sean.

Diamond bounced up and down on the chair. The people who lived below Becker began pounding on the ceiling. Finally, the knife fell out and Diamond toppled the chair.

Sean was by far a better boxer than Bruno, but the gorilla had reach, weight, and brutality on his side.

Diamond got the knife in his hand and sawed at his bonds.

Bruno was bleeding from the nose, but Sean's eye was puffy and his lip was split. Bruno connected with a freight-train hook. Sean rocked back, stunned, and Bruno wrapped him in a bone-crushing bear hug. He carried him out on the terrace.

Diamond threw the ropes off.

Sean was a limp doll in Bruno's hateful embrace. The strongarm lifted him over the railing.

Diamond seized the chair and ran to the terrace.

"Oh Brunie baby."

Bruno turned. Diamond hit him with the chair across the middle. Bruno folded, dropping Sean. The strongarm lunged. Diamond hit him with a left and a nickel-roll-bolstered right.

Bruno and Diamond struggled. The big man got Diamond in his killer bear hug. Diamond butted Bruno's broken nose. Bruno snorted and squeezed harder.

Sean got up, lifted a flower pot, and dropped it on Bruno's head. There wasn't enough force to do much damage, but the dirt got in his eyes. Sean fell over again.

Diamond swung at Bruno with all he had. Two in the breadbasket, a kick in the groin, and then an uppercut on the chin. Bruno fell back against the railing. His monstrous mitts groped for Diamond's neck. The P.I. got a grip on his legs and lifted.

It was deathly quiet on the terrace. Just Diamond and Sean and the debris from the fight.

"You . . . you killed him?" Sean asked.

"I hope so. If he comes back up, we got real problems,"

Diamond said. Although each movement hurt, he forced himself to bend and help Sean up.

They tottered into the living room where Becker lay moaning on the floor, his face as white as his hair.

Diamond took the gun Becker had been racing for and the papers. On the phone table near where Becker lay were sheets of flash paper with columns of numbers written on them. Red folded the sheets and pocketed them. A pale Sean sat stunned on the sofa.

"I hope you tipped the super good at Christmas," Diamond said to Becker. "He's got a hell of a mess to clean up off the sidewalk."

Diamond lifted the photo of Rocco with Melonie. He held it so Sean couldn't see it, but Becker could. "Who's this?"

"I don't know. She's some tramp that—"

The P.I. kicked him before he could say any more.

"Not the girl. The guy. What name is he using?"

"I don't know. You can only see his legs anyway."

Diamond shook Becker like he was a musty blanket. "What's his name?"

"I think his name is Ralph. Or Raoul."

"Or Rocco?"

"It could be."

"You bet it is. Where is he?"

"I don't know."

Diamond grabbed Becker by the scruff of his neck. "I oughta bounce you off the walls. Where do I find him?"

Becker groaned. Diamond lifted him and shoved him into a chair. "That don't sound like an address to me."

"He was visiting. From the Coast. I think."

In the distance, Diamond heard sirens.

"We better go," Sean said.

Diamond leaned over and twisted Becker's gun into his ear. "Hear me good, you lowlife bum. I took care of

57

Bruno, I'll take care of you. If Red Diamond's on your case, there's no escape. Got me?"

Becker nodded.

"Good. Tell the cops your buddy-boy accidentally did a swan dive. Otherwise, I spread the word you're cooperating with the cops. Talking to the grand jury. And that you like young ones. Even the broken-nose boys got standards."

Becker nodded again.

"If anything happens to the kid here, if he so much as gets a stomachache, I'm coming for you. Remember that."

"You gonna be okay?" Diamond asked as they walked to the car. Sean's athletic grace was gone. He was clumsy with pain and shock.

"I guess."

"First time you ever see anyone buy the farm?"

"Huh?"

"You never seen a joe get his ticket punched?"

"Excuse me?"

"Kick the bucket."

"Never."

"It's easier the second time around."

"I hope there's never a second time."

"I hope so too. Every day. Only it don't work out that way."

They got in the car.

"I feel nauseous," Sean said.

"Hold it down. You did all right. You did real good."

"You killed him. Then you threatened to kill the old man."

"He's young enough to have us thrown in the harbor with a jukebox around our necks. You gotta talk a language these animals understand."

"But would you really do that? Would you kill him in cold blood?"

Diamond lit a cigarette. "Sometimes, kid, you can really be a damned Boy Scout."

Sean's color changed rapidly. He leaned out the window and threw up.

"Don't worry about it," Diamond said, when the youth pulled his head back in. "The car was due for a wash."

On the way downtown, Sean composed himself enough for Diamond to ask how he'd avoided plunging twenty stories. Becker had had a second rope attached to Sean, tied around his waist. Bruno's rope-slicing had been strictly a way to crack Diamond. The satyr hadn't figured on Sean's gymnastic training, which allowed him to do a flip, fold himself over, and work on the knots.

"Not too shabby, if I do say so," the P.I. said.

"Thanks, Dad. What do we do next?"

"You go home and get your beauty sleep."

"Will you help me with Melonie?"

"I owe you that much."

"Great, Dad."

Diamond dropped Sean by the yellow Datsun parked near the hotel.

"So it was you tailing me," Diamond said, noticing the car.

Sean nodded. "I guess I didn't do a very good job."

"You tried. That's all you can do."

At 7:30 A.M. the next morning, the phone rang, waking Diamond.

"What did you do to him?" an agitated Tartaglia asked.

"Who?" Had Becker squealed on Red for Bruno's fall? But then the cops would've woken the P.I., not his lawyer.

"Your son."

"Oh, that kid Sean."

"Yes, that kid Sean."

"He's a good kid."

"I'm glad you like him. Then why did you beat him up?"

"What?"

"Nichols called me. He said Milly is hysterical. Sean came in last night looking like he'd been worked over. He wouldn't tell her where he'd been, but it slipped out he'd seen you. She wants to go to the police. Sean wouldn't let her. She's convinced you're a homicidal maniac."

Diamond chuckled.

"I'm beginning to wonder if she's right," Tartaglia said. "Do you mind telling me what's going on?"

"I was teaching the kid the ropes."

"How nice."

"We got the info to crack your case open."

"What's that?"

"Records of Becker's personal finances for the past six months. Plus some shots of him with girls young enough to be his granddaughters. And when they're sitting on his lap, it ain't to play Santa Claus."

"How did you get them? No, I don't want to know."

"What did you find out about this Sean and Melonie?"

"Sean is twenty-one years old, an all-around athlete. He also gets top grades in school, is popular with the coeds, member of the chess and debating teams. He's won more honors than I have time to list. Also holds down a part-time job in an electronics store."

"Jack Armstrong watch out."

"Melonie is two years younger. Her main interest seems to be boys. And men. Quite a handful. Milly blames you. Nichols said the girl didn't finish high school. Apparently, she spent some time in Puerto Rico, getting an abortion, and pregnant again. She wants to be a beautician, but Milly thinks she's using that as an excuse to buy makeup by the gallon. You know about her disappearing, I gather."

"What kind of music does she like?"

"How the hell should I know?"

"Aren't we in a good mood this morning."

"If you'd been woken by an angry shyster you'd be the same way."

"I was," Diamond said.

"Am I receiving stolen property here?" Tartaglia asked as Diamond dropped the purloined papers on his desk.

"Nah. Becker knows I took them. I was there last night."

Tartaglia held up a *News*. "Did you have anything to do with this?"

On page three there was a photo of the medical examiner's aides carrying the mortal remains of Benedict Hooper, described as a manservant for businessman and reputed crime figure Sidney Becker. Becker had suffered a heart attack, but was listed in good condition at New York Hospital. Police said Hooper had fallen off the balcony after a few drinks.

"Too bad. It's so hard to get good help nowadays."

"I got a call from one of Becker's lawyers. She asked if you were in my employ. I didn't tell her, not knowing what you had been up to."

"You want me to give the papers back?" Red said, reaching for them.

Tartaglia slapped the P.I.'s hand. "Not on your life. The lawyer was making settling noises. I think we've got them over a barrel." He picked up the flash papers.

"What's this? It feels funny."

"Flash paper, fast-burning stuff."

"Do you know what these numbers mean?"

"I was lookin' at them. Probably the tally from his policy banks. It wouldn't take the IRS very long to find out."

Diamond made sure he was far from the flash paper when he lit his cigarette.

"I spoke to Mrs. Becker this morning. She's authorized payment of five thousand dollars to you for your good work on this case," Tartaglia said.

"She knows the way to a fella's heart."

"I have another case you might—"

"Sorry, I already got another client."

"You move quick."

"It's harder to hit a moving target."

PART TWO

PART TWO

Chapter Seven

Diamond went to Palomo's near Madison Square Garden. The gym wasn't the same since it had moved from 149th Street, but it still was the best place to get the old blood running.

The pug behind the double door buzzed him in after giving him the once-over. He had the don't-trust-nobody eyes Red had seen through speakeasy peepholes.

The place smelled like the inside of a sneaker that hadn't been changed since Sugar Ray Robinson, Rocky Graziano, and Jake La Motta boxed there.

Diamond did an hour on the speed and body bags and took a hot shower. He watched the boxers work out. None of them had pro potential, or even the hope of being good club fighters. But they were young and lean and quick. He patted his spare tire without realizing it, and left before he got too envious.

Sean showed up at Diamond's hotel room late that afternoon.

"I left school early," he said. "I couldn't concentrate. I'm really worried about Melonie."

"Okay. Let's go after her. What have you checked?"

"I spoke with several of her friends. I don't think they liked me. They didn't tell me much."

"Most of the yeggs I grill don't like me. The trick is making them talk."

"But some of them were girls. I couldn't do to them what you did to Becker. Did you see the paper?"

"Only the funnies. You can make dames talk more easily. It's in their genes to yatter-chatter. You gotta know how to play 'em. You got names and addresses?"

"Sure. I have them memorized."

Diamond took out a piece of paper and pencil. "Spit 'em out and then go home and look through the phone bills. Any numbers jump out at you, give them a call. Pretend you're looking for a long-lost buddy, or selling raffle books or from the phone company."

"Maybe I could tell them the truth?"

"Save it for a last resort. Then come on strong as the grief-stricken brother. Gimme the names."

Sean recited them and where they could be reached.

"What are you going to do?"

"Visit some of Melonie's friends. You got a picture of her to show around?"

Sean handed over a high-school graduation picture that showed a prim and proper young lady in a cap and gown.

"Anything that looks more like her?"

He took out a picture of Melonie in a bikini, sunbathing in the backyard of an unappealing tract home. Diamond felt a painful twinge.

"Mmmmmmmmmmnnnnnugggh," he moaned.

"What's the matter?" Sean asked.

Red bit his lip. Melonie was definitely the girl in the photo with Rocco. But he didn't want to tell Sean that. The P.I. nodded. The dizzy spell passed.

"Maybe I should come with you," Sean suggested.

"They've already had a visit from Joe College. I can squeeze more out of them if I do like Lucky Lindy."

"What?"

"Fly solo. You go home and go through the phone records. I'll use up the shoe leather."

The P.I.'s first stop was the East Village, at a rattletrap tenement that was so shaky even demolition workers wouldn't go near it.

The front door had been ripped off its hinges, the mailboxes were crowbarred open, and there were things lying on the stair landings that Diamond didn't even want to think about.

Jerry Malle lived on the top floor. They always live on the top floor, Red thought as he trudged up the stairs. He knocked at Malle's door.

"I do not wish to be disturbed," a smooth voice with the hint of a French accent said from the other side.

Diamond stepped back and kicked the cheap door hard. It shattered quicker than the Maginot Line.

"What is zis outrage! How dare you!" Malle was a tall, scrawny pencil-neck with a cigarette drooping from insolent lips.

A nude woman lay on a couch. She wasn't hard on the eyes, but Virginia Mayo didn't have to worry.

"I told you pigs I have been clean for a month," Malle insisted.

Diamond took a few steps in. The woman's eyes had remained half-closed. As he neared her, Diamond could see the ugly mottled bruises of collapsed veins.

"Take a powder, sister," Diamond barked. She got up with difficulty and left the room without a word.

"If she's not high, I'm Dick Powell," Diamond said.

"Maybe we had a little something. To appeaze zee muze," Malle said, seeing that Diamond hadn't slapped handcuffs on. He winked. "It makes the girls more receptive. Maybe you'd like to spend time on the couch with Lily."

Diamond walked over and looked at the canvas Malle

had been working on. It was a mishmash of red, yellow, and green. "What's this?"

"That's Lily. Chicks really go for the French artist bit," Malle said, dropping his accent. "Come up to my garret and see my paintings. Get it?"

Diamond lifted it off the easel, studied it carefully, and smashed it down over the artist's head.

"I like it better this way. Now, you gonna give me some information or do I put a little more red on the canvas."

"Hey man, this is the 1980s. I wanna talk to my lawyer. I know my rights."

"You got the right to remain silent until I ask you a question. Then you got the right to answer it or eat a knuckle sandwich. You think the dames will go for you with your jaw wired shut?"

"We can make a deal."

"Answer my questions. You went out with a girl. Melonie Jaffe."

"Oh yeah. What a wild one. She could break your back."

Red didn't know why, but he pole-axed Malle. The artist fell to the floor.

"Just answer my questions. Where is she?"

"I don't know," he gasped. "We split up. I got jealous."

"What?"

"She was seeing other men."

"Who?"

"I don't know. I saw her with a few. Musicians, I guess. They were greasy-looking and carrying guitar cases."

Red didn't bother to tell him that it was probably Rocco's hit men, and the instruments in the cases only played one melody. Rat-a-tat-a-tat.

"Where'd you see them?" the P.I. asked.

"At Harvey's. The club on East Broadway."

"How long ago?"

"About three weeks ago."

Lily came into the room. "Are we gonna continue?"

"Get dressed," Diamond said. "Jerry here's got a social disease. He's gonna be quarantined for a while."

She picked up her clothes, staying as far as she could from Malle. "Why's he wearing that painting?"

"Part of the treatment," Diamond said.

"Oh." She put her clothes on and hurried out.

"What you go and do that for?" Malle whined.

"Maybe I don't like your style of painting."

Diamond breezed by the club Harvey's. It didn't open until 11 P.M. He went to check the next name on the list, Suzie Chapman. The girl was a former classmate of Melonie's, now working in a Burger Boss in Queens.

"I know you," the girl said when Diamond walked up to the counter.

"Don't believe what you read in the papers," Diamond said modestly. That was the problem with being a private eye—keeping your business private.

"For sure, you're Melonie's Pop."

Diamond didn't contradict her. It made a good cover story. "I'm looking for Melonie."

"Suzie, your line is backing up," the sharp-eyed manager shouted from the back. A six-pack of hungry patrons stood resentfully behind Diamond.

"He's been really nasty since his wife left him," Chapman whispered. "She ran off with the manager of the Hamburger House. I got a break in fifteen minutes. We can talk then."

"Fine. Meanwhile, what do you recommend?"

"The coffee shop across the street. The food is much better."

Diamond got a cup of coffee and a Hot Boss Bun and sat at a table. The bun came in a plastic container. It was hard to tell where the container ended and the food began. But the coffee was hot.

I sat in the hospital coffee shop and nursed a steaming cup of java. After a few sips, I figured out where they dumped the bedpans.

The doctor came in and sat with me. He carried a thermos with him. He shared some of his Irish coffee with me.

"How's it look?" I asked.

"Good. We stabilized her. She came out of sedation twice and asked for you. You can go in and see her in a few minutes."

"Thanks."

"How'd it happen?"

It's hard to drink with a guy and feed him a line. I told him the truth.

"She's lucky to be alive," the medico said. "So are you."

"We all are, with Rocco on the loose."

"Paging Doctor Blue. Paging Doctor Blue," the loudspeaker said. The sawbones jumped like he'd sat on a scalpel.

"Your name tag says Dr. Rankin. What's up?"

"That's the signal for a hospital-wide emergency," Rankin said confidentially.

Around us, the patients and visitors continued eating untroubled, while staff members began rushing out of the room.

"I better go with you," I said.

I followed his flapping white coat as he raced down the corridor. The staff was trying to move as quick as it could without panicking the patients. It was like half the crew of an aircraft carrier going to battle stations while the other half went about their business.

The chief administrator was an elderly gal with hair in a tight bun and a clipboard pressed against her bosom.

"What's going on?" Rankin asked.

"A bomb has been planted in the building. It's set to go off in ten minutes."

"Not enough time to evacuate," another doc said needlessly.

"Who would do such a thing?"

"The caller said unless we leave one of our patients out by the loading dock for him, the whole building will go up."

"Which patient?" a dame with high heels and a higher hairdo asked.

"Fifi La Roche," the administrator said.

"Rocco," I shouted, and everyone looked at me.

"Who are you?" the administrator demanded.

"I'm the hawkshaw that's gonna solve your problem," I told her. "I got an idea."

"Mr. Jaffe, Mr. Jaffe."

A hand touched Diamond's shoulder, and he snapped back to the Burger Boss.

"The coffee get to you?"

"Nah, I'm fine, sit down."

"I can only talk for a few minutes. At Burger Boss School they teach that five minutes is the optimum break time. It gives you just enough time to stretch, go to the bathroom, and blink a few times."

"That's a tough break."

She mooched one of Diamond's cigarettes. She had bright blue eyes that would take in a lot, and a wide mouth that would make sure to report what she saw.

"I used to be able to sneak more time. But Stu, he's got a second job. He bought a car and he can't make the payments, so he's working—"

"Melonie's disappeared," Diamond interrupted. "I'm trying to find her."

"I haven't seen her in months. Your son was by. He's smart and radically cute. I don't care if he's snooty. Do you know if he has a girlfriend? What's he interested in?"

"I don't know. What can you tell me about Melonie?"

"I shouldn't tell you this, you being her father," Chapman said.

"Her life may depend on it. I can take it."

The floodgates opened as Chapman got a chance to do some first-class gossiping. She detailed Melonie's boyfriends and love life, including details graphic enough to make Red uncomfortable.

". . . but she dumped him when he wanted her to get friendly first with his twin sister. Then she was with—"

"I only need to know the most recent ones."

"There was an artist, lived in a total dump. I've seen better art in the subways. He's just a barfbag trying to pick up girls."

"I agree. Anyone else?"

"I got this second-hand, so I can't really say, but I heard she was with Spit."

"What?"

"Spit. He's the lead singer with Crippled Nipples."

"What's that?"

"A heavy metal band. They used to be pretty bitchin'. They're yesterday's news."

"Suzie, you're on duty," the manager called out.

"He has no right to be so fussy about the rules. I know he's pocketing petty cash," she told Diamond. "But I need the job. You know, Melonie described you as a wimp."

She got up. "I think she was wrong, though."

"Is that right?"

"You're not a wimp."

"Thanks."

"Suzie, you're going to be docked," the manager said.

She wrinkled her nose and stuck out her tongue, but did it so that Red, and not the manager, saw it. "Listen, when you find out what happens, will you tell me? I mean, I can keep a secret."

72

"If I find out anything, I'll definitely consider telling you," Diamond said.

She hurried back to the counter.

I'll consider it the way I consider playing Russian roulette with an automatic, Red thought, as he finished his coffee and hit the streets.

Chapter Eight

Diamond checked out two more names on the list. Neither of them provided any help.

The woman—an overdressed twenty-one-year-old with the charm of an open wound—tried to sell him provocative men's briefs. The man said he was a law student studying for the bar. He threatened to sue Diamond for breaking his concentration. Diamond offered to break his leg as well, and the attorney-to-be slammed the door in his face.

The P.I. drove back to Harvey's.

There was a line outside of joes and janes with equally long hair, black leather, metal chokers, and wristlets. Despite their tough trappings, most looked like spoiled middle-class kids from the suburbs.

"This isn't a Lawrence Welk concert," a leather-vested youth with a caved-in chest sneered when Diamond got on line. His girlfriend, whose chest was no bigger, tittered.

Diamond ignored him. Others waiting egged Vest on.

"I think you're underage. You have proof you're old enough?" Vest asked.

The line had stopped moving forward. Diamond lit a cigarette and waited.

"You can't smoke here," Vest said to Diamond, although many of the people were burning either tobacco or

Mary Jane. He punched Red's arm. "Old man, what's wrong with your hearing?"

Diamond spun and pulled Vest toward him by his hair. He puffed on the cigarette, then held its red-hot tip under Vest's nose. "You want me to put it out?"

"Like wow, no, I mean, I was only kidding."

Diamond let go of Vest, who cringed against the wall. The toughly attired punks had vanished. Diamond was at the front of the line.

"Gimme one," he said to the purple-haired girl in the ticket booth.

She took his money and slid him his ticket. "You sure you want to go in? It ain't your kind of music, pops."

"Ain't Lawrence Welk performing tonight?"

Before she could answer, he was inside.

Lights flashed in the smoky haze and bizarre figures contorted on the dance floor. But the noise coming from the stage overwhelmed rival sensations.

Diamond couldn't understand what the four scrawny youths on stage were shrieking. The lead singer was the most conservatively dressed, with black leather pants and a metal-studded codpiece. He was yowling something like "Satan, take my mother 'cause I wanna party tonight."

The others were wearing more makeup than clothing. Their amplified electric instruments were louder than a Panzer division on the blitz.

The P.I. eased through the crowd of kids, who bobbed like corks on a musical sea. The heavy metal fans moved out of his way. Word about the incident on line had spread, and Diamond cut a conspicuous figure as he pressed toward the front of the theater.

He entered a side door and ran into the stage manager.

"You can't come back here," the manager said. He had steel-gray hair and dark, friendly eyes, despite his words.

"Who's in charge around here?"

75

"Of what? If you're here to pay for a rental, me. If you want to hire the creeps on stage, Jack Sharkey. He handles this group and a slew of other morons in the business. If you're from the Health Department, Fire Marshal's, or any collection agency, the boss is on vacation."

Diamond grunted as the band hit a particularly offensive high note. "The Glenn Miller Band these petunias ain't."

The stage manager grinned and waved for Diamond to follow him into a soundproofed room behind the stage. The walls were covered with photos of the big-band greats, all autographed to Chuck Maher.

"I was in Jersey with Harry James when he discovered Sinatra," Maher said when he saw Diamond admiring his collection. "I was with him and the Music Makers for ten years. I was there when Artie Shaw met Ava Gardner, when Freddy Martin first played 'Tonight We Love' at the Ritz Carlton. But you're too young to remember."

"How about Martin at the Waldorf doing 'Louisiana Hayride,' with Jerry Colonna and Tommy Dorsey making sweet sounds in the trombone section?"

"I got the original Brunswick recording at home. And Benny Goodman doing 'Sing, Sing, Sing' at Carnegie Hall."

Diamond nodded, properly appreciative.

For ten minutes, they chatted about the big-band sound. By the time Diamond got down to business, it was like they were old friends.

"Ever seen this girl around?" Diamond asked, holding up the picture of Melonie and the man's legs.

"I tell you, they all start to look the same," Maher said. "He's built kind of small."

"You know him?"

"Musicians have always been a little more wild than other folks," he continued, without hearing Diamond. "So

76

they have girlfriends. Maybe smoke a little tea. But nowadays—" Maher made a clucking noise of disapproval. "How the hell could I tell from looking at his pecker? But I think I seen her. With a screecher named Spit. Spit the twit, I call him. But the girlies like him."

"Know where I can get ahold of him?"

"He's managed by the same guy as this group of tone-deaf twerps. I'll introduce you to Sharkey. I didn't catch your name?"

"Red Diamond. I'm a private eye."

"The name's familiar. Seems like I read it somewhere. You ever been written up?"

"Yeah."

"I thought so. I better warn you, Sharkey don't like P.I.'s. His boys have been hit with paternity suits."

"How about you don't tell him what I do?"

"Sure. He's a jerk too. He pretends this crap is music, passing this amplified cat-wailing off on dumb kids who don't know better."

Maher winked and opened the door. The music hit them like the backwash from a DC-3. They walked backstage, past roadies sitting on assorted amplifying gear, groupies preening, and guards straining to keep back adoring fans.

Sharkey was in his late forties, heavyset, and sweating profusely. He stood out, dressed like Diamond, in a sport jacket and slacks. The pale green tie around his neck looked like wilted celery.

Sharkey was nodding to the music and watching the audience with cash-register eyes. He spotted Maher and waved. Maher signaled that he wanted to talk.

They walked back to the dressing room, which wasn't soundproofed, but far enough away from the stage that the noise was a dulled roar and thump.

"Aren't they great?" Sharkey asked as he burst in and lit the first of a dozen cigarettes he'd chainsmoke.

77

"Who?" Diamond asked.

"Crush."

"The jerks out on stage," Maher said.

"Jerks? You see the house tonight. It's filled. Bad Noose couldn't do that. Grim Reapers couldn't do that. Jet Engine couldn't do that."

"Just because people eat horsemeat it don't mean it's filet mignon," Maher said. He turned to Diamond. "Would you believe this character has degrees from Juilliard and Harvard Business School, and he spends his time selling crappy noise to teenagers?"

Sharkey turned to Diamond and acted as if Maher wasn't in the room. "I heard about you."

"Word travels fast," Diamond said coolly.

"Fast enough. Would you like a job?"

"I got one. What did you hear?"

"About the incident out front. You scared the bejesus out of the kids. My main security man is going away."

"Going away is right," Maher chimed in. "He's gonna be a guest of the government. Up at Sing Sing."

"It was a bad rap and you know it," Sharkey said. "That kid deserved to be hit."

"But not with a two-by-four," Maher responded.

"I want someone older," Sharkey said. "With a bit more restraint."

"He's got more restraint," Maher said, nodding at Diamond. "Attila the Hun's got more restraint."

"Chuck, don't you have some light bulbs to change somewhere?" Sharkey asked. "Let me talk with Mister . . . Mister. . . ?"

"Diamond, Red Diamond."

Chuck walked out muttering.

"What do you do, Red?"

"Whatever I can. A little of this, a little of that."

"Much call for your work?"

"Enough to keep me off the breadlines," Diamond

said, taking out the picture of Melonie and Rocco's lower half. "Recognize either of these?"

"No," he said, without looking. "I don't need any grief. You're not welcome here."

"Listen, Jackie, you can give me the bum's rush if you want. But I got friends. I bet the Fire Department would like to check your permits for the smudge pots you got out there. How many of those girls backstage drinking are underage? If a coupla narcs went through your equipment, you think they'd be happy with what they found?"

"It's not my responsibility to see—"

"I don't give a damn whose responsibility it is. All I care about is the picture. I know the girl was going with Spit. So if you want to play somebody for a chump, better find a P.I. who don't know shit from shinola. But that ain't me."

The manager looked at the photo. "Okay. I've seen her. Maybe two, three weeks ago. I heard she was splitting for the Coast. Listen, I don't want any trouble."

"There won't be any. I was hired to make sure she's doing whatever she's doing with a free will. If she is, I leave her. If she's being forced to do anything she don't want, then I bust heads."

"That's fair. Are you positive you wouldn't like to work for me? I have one of the largest independent personal and business management firms in the entertainment industry. I could throw you plenty of business."

"I couldn't take the noise."

"Not with this group. I got a band out in Los Angeles. Peter Piper and the Pickled Peppers. They've been getting threats. One of them died last week."

"Sounds like police business to me."

"The police ruled it accidental. They didn't look very hard. Peter has a way of getting on people's nerves."

"Most of my clients do. That's why they need me. I give lessons on how to be lovable."

79

"The group is as popular with the fuzz as Jane Fonda is with the American Legion. They released several songs in the sixties that the cops still remember. Like 'Kill the Porkers' and 'Badges, Blood, and Brutality of the Fascist Fuzz.'"

"Real catchy titles."

"Number one with a bullet for seven weeks on the nationwide chart. They've got a comeback album in the works that's gonna go platinum, no ifs, ands, or buts."

"What kind of threats did they get?"

"The latest was a phone call. On my unlisted number. A woman said, 'They will die,' and that was it."

"Not very impressive. No demands for money, or credit, or blaming your boys for the coming end of the world?"

Sharkey shook his head. "I've been in this business for years. I've seen lots of rock stars drop dead before their time. No one has ever done squat about it."

Sharkey, with a cigarette still in his mouth, went to light another. He laughed nervously when he saw his mistake. "I'll make you a deal. This girl you're looking for is out there. Spit wants to quit the performing end and go into production. She went with him. He's trying to hammer out a deal with Vine-L Records. You go, look into my problem, *then* find the girl. I'll pay your usual rates, plus a hundred bucks a day."

"You sold me," Diamond said. "Make up quickie files on the players so I know who's who."

"You got it. When you get out there, talk to Ted Kirk. He owns Vine-L."

"What's that?"

"The record company that's doing the boys' latest album. Ted's been around for years. He's a creep and a crook, but he knows the business. He invented payola. And pioneered kickbacks on the TV show 'Rock Premier.' He was the first to figure out a way to make bribes tax deductible."

"Sounds like the Thomas Edison of sleaze."

"I trust him as far as I can throw him, but he gets things done."

"So does Mussolini."

"Does? You mean did, don't you?" Sharkey said, handing the photo back to Diamond. The P.I. left without answering.

"But we're not certain she's in California," Sean said through the phone.

"All roads point there, kid. Besides, I got to get back and clean up my junk mail."

"Can I come with you?"

"You have school."

"I can take a leave."

"Stay in school or you might wind up a busted-down peeper."

"But Dad—" Sean complained.

"No buts. And no Dads. Can't you call me Red?"

"I'll try, Da——Red."

"Keep your chin up. I'm not running out on your case. I told you Red Diamond don't do that. With a paying client to foot the bill, I can get a lot more done, travel more, grease the wheels if I have to."

"What if she's still in New York?"

"You got to trust your instincts. My nose is pointing to L.A. Don't worry, I'm on the case," the P.I. said, hanging up before Sean had a chance to challenge him further.

"Miss La Roche, you know you're risking your life by leaving the hospital," Dr. Rankin said.

"Didn't you say the other patients could be hurt if I didn't?" she asked in that sexy little-girl voice of hers.

81

He nodded.

"Then let's go. Besides, Red can take better care of me than a hospital full of doctors. No offense meant."

"None taken," he said.

What a dame! I thought, and I could see the medico was feeling the same way. A heart of gold and a body that was even more valuable. She made a hospital smock look like one of them fancy designer dresses.

I could see the doc was wishing that she'd give her body to science. But I knew she was saving it for me. The medical team prepped her and wheeled the gurney to the elevator.

"Are you sure you want to go through with it?" the head administrator broad asked. "We are used to saving lives here, not putting them in jeopardy."

"I guess you never ate in the cafeteria," I cracked. "Keep the chin up, buttercup. Fifi and me have been in tougher scrapes. Where's a better place to get shot than a hospital?"

Rankin led me to the doctor's dressing room. We picked out a gown that left me enough room to grab my piece without surgery. He put a cap on my noodle and a gauze mask over my face.

He draped a stethoscope around my neck. "This is my good-luck charm. I've had it since med school."

I gave him a simple thanks, but he didn't have to be a cardiac specialist to know it came from the heart.

Then I was wheeling my luscious lovely down the hall as the hands on the wall clocks ticked like crows pecking at a gravestone.

"I'm scared, Red," she said.

"Stop shaking, baby, you're distracting me from my work."

"Oh, you're such an animal. I love it."

I didn't get a chance to answer. A black Packard drove up, screeching like a society dame who spotted a mouse in her mousse.

82

Two of Rocco's boys extricated themselves and shoved me aside. "All right, sawbones, we'll take over."

They snatched Fifi and hustled her into the car. I could see Rocco's leering puss inside.

"What about the bomb?" I asked, trying to make my voice sound doctorlike.

"In the basement, near the oxygen tanks."

They hopped in the car. It hadn't worked out like I'd hoped. There was no way to get a clear shot without perforating my pretty pumpkin.

I ran to the hospital entrance. "In the basement, near the oxygen tanks."

I heard Rankin yelling directions to the police bomb squad, which was just speeding up. I ran to Rocco's car. I reached in and snatched the keys.

The goons got out, ready to earn their keep on an out-of-his-league doctor. The first came at me baring sharp yellow teeth, like an ugly Doberman guarding a fresh bone. I used the butt of the roscoe to do a little dental work.

The second goon lunged and swung a few good ones, knocking the mask from my face.

"It's Diamond," he gasped.

While he was IDing me, I was KOing him. Shocked, he stood in place for a picture-perfect combination that would've done Dempsey proud.

The engine started. Rocco must've had a spare set of keys. I jumped on the hood as he took off. He braked and swerved, shaking the car like a jitterbugger with ants in his pants.

I hung on, blocking his view by laying my carcass across the windshield.

He poked his head out to see where he was going. I planted a few jabs with my right, while clinging to the car with my left. They weren't enough to hurt him, but they made him lose control and he slammed the car into a hydrant. Water came gushing up like Old Faithful.

He staggered out of the car, with his grubby paws around my frail. He had a gun to her head and a determined gleam in his eye.

"This is it, shamus, for you and the dame."

Suddenly, he yowled like he'd sat on a porcupine. Fifi had made good use of the scalpel we'd taped to her succulent forearm. She'd planted it right in Rocco's thigh. I thought my babe's aim was a little low, but he had gotten the point.

She slipped away and we stood face-to-face. Me and Rocco. Rocco the white-slaver, drug dealer, arms smuggler, government corrupter, baby-killer, mass-murderer.

"You wouldn't shoot a fella that doesn't have a chance, would you?"

"You had your chance. And every chance you had you did rotten," I said.

"I can make you rich and powerful."

The gun in my hand punctuated Rocco's last sentence. Fifi was close to me. I could smell her lush scent.

"Fasten your seat belt, honey, we're coming in for a landing," she said.

Chapter Nine

It wasn't Fifi, only a stewardess with blond hair who leaned over the daydreaming Red as the plane swung wide over L.A.

"Do you make housecalls?" he asked.

She clicked the seat belt in his lap, smiled professionally, and moved on.

Driving from the airport, Red thought of the files he'd been reviewing on the plane. Sharkey had put together a packet on the band, although much of it was press-agent puffery, as worthless as a recruiting sergeant's promises.

There were three members of the band. They had met at a clinic in Haight-Ashbury in 1964. Lead singer Peter Piper was getting penicillin shots for a venereal disease. Drummer Charlie Wynn was being treated for a drug overdose, and lead guitarist Wyatt Edwards was working as a volunteer counselor.

Piper and Edwards came from wealthy backgrounds— Wynn was a scrapper from a blue-collar family. In the sixties, they preferred tents to motels. In the seventies, they stayed in motels, and tore rooms apart. Now they owned a motel chain. And they're finicky about who they take in, Sharkey wrote.

"Their music has always been full of energy, very contemporary," a critic said. "They have ridden each wave, each trend with the assuredness of champion surfers. Their new album promises to be a breakthrough. They have the longevity of the Rolling Stones, the presence of Michael Jackson, and the creativity of the Beatles. Their rock video, depicting the group conquering an army of Amazons in outer space, has the technical superiority of a feature film."

Little mention was made of the musicians who filled the rest of the slots—keyboard, bass guitar, backup vocals, saxophone—and came and went with the Pickled Peppers' needs.

Diamond stopped off in his office on Hollywood Boulevard near Ivar, in the aging Carlin Building. The landlord tried to convince the tenants it was a quaint landmark and they should be paying more rent. Diamond tried to convince his clients it wasn't a decaying deathtrap.

The office had the musty confined smell of unemptied ashtrays, stale air, and no business. Diamond put the bios in the top drawer of the file cabinet.

He used his Polaroid copying attachment to make dupes of the photo of Melonie and Rocco's lower half. The camera came in handy when he didn't want photo clerks to know what he was up to and he needed duplicates in a hurry. He snapped off five shots of the photo and set them out on his blotter to dry.

He caught up on his mail and phone messages. Bills, bills, bills, and an announcement that he may have won a million dollars, but if he ordered books from Publisher's Bonanza, he could never lose. Another firm offered him a free gift, either a car, a stereo, or a plastic grandfather clock, if he came out and viewed their desert land, which was soon going to be worth more than Malibu beachfront property.

The bills went in a drawer, the junk mail went in the circular file. The answering service had only taken messages for his first three days away. They had cut off service for lack of payment.

Diamond went to the bank and deposited the money from Mrs. Becker and the retainer from Sharkey, paid the bills, and went home to do battle with his jet lag.

His apartment was on Fountain Avenue, in a building that looked like a castle and had fixtures dating back to King George. The place came furnished—the only things that belonged to him were the old hi-fi in the corner and the two dozen records by big-band greats. He put an Artie Shaw platter on the turntable, and "Frenesi" filled the room.

He snagged a bottle of bourbon from the shelf and sank down in a chair that looked like it had been mauled by a panther. He didn't care how shabby his place was. Red Diamond alone was not a homebody. Not until he found his Fifi. Then he'd build a nest.

I'd spent hours at my doll's bedside, making goo-goo eyes at her while she slept unaware.

I'd watched the color return to her smooth cheeks, both sets. On the day she walked out, I gave her a fancy dress that cost a bundle at a store where the sales help talked like they were British royalty working part-time.

She loved it, but refused to try it on until we got someplace cozy. I knew just the place.

Hodel's Motel. I had saved the brothers who owned the place once from a gang of zoot-suiters with trouble on their minds. They were setting mattresses on fire. Only problem was, customers were in them at the time.

I had given the zoot-suiters a dozen .38 caliber button holes. The Hodels had given me a standing invite.

They prepared the room like the presidential suite at the Waldorf. Champagne in a silver ice bucket, more flowers than at Dion O'Banion's funeral, a bed the size of a basketball court, Les Brown's "Sentimental Journey" softly playing on the cathedral radio, hoity-toity art prints on the walls.

But the most beautiful thing in the room was the one hundred and ten pounds of gal flesh that came bouncing out of the bathroom in the white-and-black silk number I'd dropped my hard-earned shekels for.

"Oh, Red. It's beautiful."

"It don't do you justice," I said, though my optics were working overtime to take in the view.

"Do you like it?" she asked, doing a pirouette just out of reach.

"I'd like nothing better."

The dress slid down like butter off a hot plate. I'd checked it out with the salesgirl at the store. She was a cute petit four who'd giggled when I'd asked. But she'd been right.

I nibbled Fifi's ear like it was a piece of sweet corn, then traveled down her neck.

"Red, oh Red," was all she could say, but her arms squeezing me close said more than a Winston Churchill speech.

She was wearing a black silk chemise that had the pleasure of clinging tight to her body. I began making plans to replace it. I killed the lights. The glow from the radio's tubes was the only thing to break the darkness.

We danced without moving as Helen O'Connell sang "Embraceable You."

"We been apart so long," Fifi said, fingering my shirt buttons.

I carried her to the bed.

"We got time to make up for lost time, dollface."

It seemed like days later, but the clock promised it was only five hours when Red got up and made a cup of instant. The water pumped out of the rusty tap with the enthusiasm of a kid on his way to the first day of school.

He found a can of franks and beans in the cupboard, heated it on the gas range, and chowed down without bothering to use a plate. Red couldn't complain—the spoon was clean. Which was more than he could say about most of the joints he ate in.

He called Vine-L Records and got Kirk's secretary. She had a cultured voice and an abrupt manner. She did everything but hang up to get rid of him. The P.I. finally convinced her to put him through.

Kirk's voice was pure Brooklyn, and he came across like Diamond's long-lost uncle.

"So, you know Sharkey. A close personal friend of mine, and a truly wonderful human being. How is he? It's been too long. I don't get to New York as much as I would like to. Such great delis. You ever go to Katz's? How about the pizza at Ray's? Or Junior's cheesecake? But enough of that, how can I help you? Any friend of Sharkey's is a friend of mine."

"I'm looking into Wyatt Edwards's death."

"Uhhhhhh. That old thing. Is Sharkey still going around saying that boy was murdered? I tell you, you're better off letting sleeping dogs lie."

"I been hired to do a job, Mr. Kirk. I'd like your help, but I'll look into it one way or the other."

"Okay, okay. Why don't you come by the office? I got copies of the police reports here. You can take a look and see what you think. I'd like to meet you."

Vine-L's headquarters was in a three-story building on Cahuenga. It had gone up in the era when hot-dog stands looked like frankfurters, photo stores were shaped like cameras, and florists' outlets were built like flower pots. It had belonged to a doughnut store.

Diamond entered the hole in the middle and found the hall to Kirk's office. The secretary, a strawberry blond who looked cold enough to chill a polar bear, ordered Diamond to wait in the foyer.

There was a couch that tried to swallow all two hundred pounds of the P.I. He scanned the old copies of *Billboard, Cashbox,* and *Rolling Stone* left on the adjacent table, waiting fifteen minutes before the secretary came for him.

Kirk was on the phone, talking about distribution rights to a record that was out-of-print. He waved for Diamond to sit. The P.I. tested the chair to make sure it wouldn't gobble him down.

He decided it was relatively safe and sat facing Kirk's cluttered, bed-size desk. Diamond couldn't read any of the memos, so he turned his attention to the room. On the walls were framed gold and platinum records, and lots of photos of Kirk with smirking, long-haired young men.

". . . top of the charts. It's time for the public to recognize what I been seeing for years. Love you too, baby. Have your girl call my girl and we'll take lunch. *Ciao.*"

The record-company owner was capped by a bad toupee that rested on big ears. He had the habit of pulling at the right lobe, and it was slightly longer than the left. He firmly shook Diamond's paw with his own manicured hands.

"So, Mr. Diamond, what do you think?"

"About what?"

"This building. I bought it for a song fifteen years ago." Kirk waited. "Get it, bought it for a song. I'm in the music business, you know."

"I know. Don't try going into comedy."

"Why the tough-guy act?"

"It's no act. When I start a case, I don't get too chummy with nobody. Look at my buddy Spade. He got too tight with Brigid, then he had to send her up for murder."

"Your buddy Spade? You mean you like reading about him?"

"Nah. I don't bother reading much of the junk that gets written about my friends. Like Marlowe. That

90

Chandler was a weirdo. Wore white gloves, like Mickey Mouse. He was a Brit, too. Or Hammer. Spillane was all right to knock around with, till he got religion."

"Ohhhh. I see," Kirk said, nodding understandingly. "I have to make a quick phone call."

Diamond lit up while Kirk dialed. "Yeah, Jackie, Hi. There's a Red Diamond here. Did you send him? . . . Right, a full deck . . . What do you mean that's just what Peter and the Peppers need? All artists are like that . . . I see . . . Well, if anything happens, it's on your head."

Kirk got off, all synthetic smiles. "You sure you want this case? Maybe you should take a long rest for a while. I know a place in Ojai where—"

"You keep trying to put me off. You covering up something?"

Kirk sighed and took a six-page police report from his desk. "Why don't you read through this and see if you still think it was murder?"

The record mogul made calls and reviewed papers. His secretary came in twice with messages.

"You couldn'ta hired her for her smiling face," Diamond said after the second time.

"Alice is great at keeping out the oddballs," Kirk said. Then he looked at the P.I. and tugged his ear. "I mean the oddballs I don't want to see. You got a lot of tone-deaf people think they're Paul McCartney. These ears of mine are worth millions. I can't waste them on off-key yowling."

Diamond went back to his papers:

At 1800 hours on Saturday, February 16, Wyatt James Edwards (M/W 40) had been found dead on the floor of his residence at 1300 Surfview Lane in Malibu. His live-in girlfriend Debbie Baker (F/W) found him in the living room of premises with fresh needle marks on his arms. Baker, who had been with Edwards for six years, said she did not know of any drug use by him. Baker, it was verified, was shopping on Rodeo Drive at the approximate time of death.

Sheriff's deputy homicide investigator Bruce Henderson had also interviewed Charlie Wynn, Ted Kirk, and Penelope Chance, the band's producer, on their most recent three albums.

The subjects expressed surprise at the death and its cause. Peter Piper "refused to be interviewed by deposing officer because said officer is 'an oppressive fascist tool.'" Henderson noted Piper complained about fascist oppression from the Olympic-size swimming pool of his fourteen-room mansion in Brentwood.

The report suggested a coroner's inquest. Attached was the initial coroner's report, which concluded that the death was accidental, and a memo signed by the undersheriff rejecting the request for an inquest.

"See. An open-and-shut case," Kirk said when Diamond looked up.

"Why are you so eager to have it closed?"

"Me. I want justice to be done. Will justice be done if there's bad publicity right before the album comes out? Will justice be done if the police start sticking their noses into our business? Will justice be done if the rest of the group, who were broken up when this horrible thing happened, are questioned and upset again so that they can't be in the recording studio where they're working on their biggest and best album ever?" He paused for air.

"What kind of music do they do?"

"Where have you been the past twenty years? Haven't you heard their music? They were chartbusters in the sixties. They slowed a little in the seventies. Now they're gonna be big again. I'll have Alice give you their records on the way out. You can listen and decide."

"You got any Eddy Duchin?"

"I can get some for you. I can do lots for my friends. So, after reading that report, don't you think you can just take it easy? Lie on the beach. I know a coupla cuties who'd love to meet a real private eye. Then tell Sharkey you couldn't find anything."

Diamond got up. "Thanks for your time. I'll speak to the group and see what there is to see."

"Suit yourself," Kirk said, tugging at his ear.

"I always do."

A dapper, slender thirty-year-old in a gray suit was seated in the Venus's-flytrap couch as Diamond left Kirk's office. He was clean-shaven with short brown hair and clear blue eyes.

"You can go in now, Spit," the secretary said to him.

As the man got up, Diamond slugged him in the gut, and dragged him outside. The secretary looked on, too stunned to scream.

"You're Spit, huh?" Diamond asked, slamming him against the building. They were in the rear parking lot, out of view of passersby. Diamond took out the photo of Melonie. "Where is she? If I don't like the answer, I'm gonna pulverize you."

"I don't know, honest," Spit said, his eyes watery.

"You don't look like what I imagined," Diamond said, releasing his grip on Spit's lapels. "What about the girl?"

"I came out here with her."

"That's a Mann Act violation right there."

"What? What did I do?"

"That's what I want to know, pretty boy."

"My intentions were honorable. The sleazoid rap was hype. I'd much rather sit in front of a fireplace than bite the heads off frogs. Honestly. I'm into management now. I've got two groups I'm promoting and—"

"I don't wanna know the story of your life. Just hers."

"We were living together in Marina del Rey. I was still doing the heavy metal trip, which followed the New Wave scene, which followed the punk—"

"Shut up and get to the point."

93

"I was souring on the whole lifestyle, the girls tearing at my clothes every night, the crappy interviews with dumb-ass reporters, the parties I had to go to, where cocaine was served like cheese-dip, the—"

"Yeah, I know, life is tough."

"She loved all of that. When I started skipping bashes, she started going out on the town without me. She hooked up with a sharp operator she had met back east. That's all I know of him."

"Is this him?" Diamond demanded, pointing to the legs in the photo.

"I don't know. I never saw him naked. That's not even his whole body."

Diamond pocketed the photo. "All right."

"She wasn't a bad kid. If there's anything I can do, give me a call," Spit said, scrawling his home phone number on the back of his business card.

Around the corner of the building, two billyclub-toting security guards, led by Alice the secretary, came hurrying.

"There they are," she said, and the guards rushed Diamond.

The P.I. took out his .38. The rent-a-cops froze with clubs in the air.

"It's okay, Alice," Spit said. "We worked everything out."

The guards were only too happy to have an excuse to back off. Spit put his arm around the distraught secretary and led her back into the building.

Chapter Ten

The most meat on drummer Charlie Wynn's body was in his generous nose. He was six feet tall and no more than 150 pounds, a mass of lean sinews, tight muscles, and bulging arteries. His skin was a taut canvas stretched across the various cables that kept his body running.

And running it was. Wynn had agreed to be interviewed by Diamond, but only had time to talk if Diamond would jog along with him during his daily run.

Wynn hadn't spoken for two miles, insisting on concentrating on his form. Then they were on San Vicente, passing other joggers in various states of exhaustion. Diamond was panting. Wynn wasn't even sweating.

"So, what do you want to know?" Wynn asked.

"Edwards. Do you think he was killed?"

"It's hard to say. If anyone knows what dopers are like, it's me. He wasn't."

"Why?" Diamond asked, trying to keep his questions short to conserve his breath.

"He didn't have the attitude. Sure he smoked grass. Priests smoke grass. Police chiefs smoke grass. They don't realize how it robs the body of nutrients. It might even do more damage than tobacco. It irritates tissues. Makes you eat too much."

Wynn increased his pace. "Wyatt's biggest problem was he was in love with a bitch. I think he would've OD'd deliberately if she told him to."

"Did she?"

"I doubt it. She's too smart to derail the gravy train."

"Enemies?"

"Some people thought he'd sold out. Radicals he used to be chummy with were always contacting him, asking him for money, favors. He gave away hundreds of thousands to charities. Some were legit, some were hustlers. He didn't care. He thought money could cure everything."

"Uhhhhh," Diamond grunted.

"It can't. Discipline. That's the answer. You have to take control of your life. You know about INO?"

"Uhhhh?"

"I'm Number One. INO. The path to accepting responsibility. It's a way of life, a philosophy, a religion for our times."

"Was that one of the crackpot charities Edwards gave to?"

Wynn glared at Diamond and began running even faster. "In centuries to come, INO will be appreciated. Superior people will take control of their destinies. They can then help shape the future. I was a drug user myself. Now I've purified my body and mind. Just the way one day I'll help to purify the world."

"I knew a, uh, uh, German paperhanger once had similar ideas."

A few beads of sweat had appeared on Wynn's brow as he zipped along. Diamond wheezed, gasped, and panted, but refused to give up.

"Who, uhhhh, got, uuuhhh, money?"

"The only one who got on a regular basis was Eddie Ross. He's got a skate stand over in Venice. Rolling Ross."

"I better go see him right away."

"Can't take the pace I've set?"

"Yeah, you're holding me back."

Wynn loped off. Diamond leaned against a sign post and heaved for ten minutes. He walked back to his car and drove to Venice.

Rolling Ross was a rolypoly man behind the counter of a wooden stand just off the Venice speedway. SKATE RENTAL BY THE HOUR OR DAY, RIDE FOR HEALTH, RIDE FOR PLAY, the sign across the roof said.

Two cute teenage girls, with perfect bottoms molded by skintight short shorts, were getting skates. Ross, bushy, bearded, with a Dodgers baseball cap perched on frizzy hair, flirted with them.

California girls, Red thought, blond, beautiful, and bouncy. Of course the best of them didn't hold a candle to one lock of Fifi's hair.

"Ohhhhh, Red," Fifi said, throwing a thigh across me and snuggling against my chest. "That was incredible."

"I know what you're talking about, angel. I was there too." I puffed on my tobacco stick and stared at the ceiling, letting my body melt into the bed.

Her fingertips traced their way across my bare flesh as Charlie Barnet's "Cherokee" played in the background. "You're such a savage, Red."

"Only for a tomato like you."

In the darkness I could make out the outline of her shape. I liked what I saw. She had mountains where other gals had hills, and valleys where others had ditches. I wished I was the kinda mug who was good with words, rather than my fists, so I could do the doll justice.

But she didn't care. I was saying what we was feeling with my voice box silent and my lips against hers.

"Ohhhh, Red," she crooned, and I knew we were off on Round Four.

* * *

"Hey mojo, you gonna stand there all day or you want to rent a pair of skates?" The dulcet tones Ross had used when bantering with the teen skaters was gone.

The nubile teens had rolled away while Red daydreamed. "I hear you were a friend of Wyatt Edwards."

Ross was suddenly somber. "I was more than a friend. I was his conscience. What's it to you?"

"I'm a dick, looking into his death."

"I thought the cops closed the case?"

"They did. I'm private. Working for Sharkey."

"Good. The thing stinks. He wouldn't take drugs. At least not to overdose. He had his head on his shoulders."

"I heard he was giving you money."

"Not me personally. I was a funnel. I handled his charities. Youth centers, drug rehab clinics, handicapped training groups, community development. He was a good man. Wyatt put about two million back in the community."

"And you handled it all?"

"Don't let this little stand throw you. I was summa cum laude from UCLA Law School. I know how to set up a trust fund or a foundation as well as the best Wilshire Boulevard lawyer," Ross said. "Now I got a question for you. Did you sit in a sauna in that outfit?"

The sweat he'd worked up was beginning to dry, and gave Red a chill from the sea breezes.

"I was running with Charlie Wynn."

"The fitness fascist. Mandatory vitamins for the Third World. He tell you his theories?"

Diamond shook his head and lit a cigarette.

"He believes they're backward because of nutritional deficiencies. If he has his way everyone more than five pounds overweight will be sent to fitness detention centers, for dietary retraining. And don't ever smoke in front of him."

Red unconsciously patted his belly. "Sounds like you don't like him?"

"Edwards was the only one worth more than a bucket of sea slugs. Penelope Chance's okay too. You met her yet?"

Diamond shook his head.

"A knockout blond. But she's not one of these bubbleheads with an IQ equal to her boob size. She's a sharp customer. You see her, tell her I said hello."

"I'll do that." Diamond took out the photo of Melonie. "Seen her around?"

"She connected with Wyatt's death?"

"Nah. A favor I'm doing for someone. Runaway."

"I might be able to find out something. I got lots of contacts. You want to leave the pix with me?"

"Sure," Diamond handed it over. "I'm interested in the hairbag too."

"Not much to go by."

"His name's Rocco Rico. Might be using the name Ralph. Or Raoul."

"Don't know him offhand."

"One last question, can you think of any enemies Wyatt might've had?"

"He was in the public eye for two decades, so you never know. Look at John Lennon. Everyone who knew Wyatt liked him. You won't find anyone to say a bad word about him."

"Wyatt Edwards was a prick," Debbie Baker said, leaning back on a couch as big as a Cadillac. She was wearing a slit skirt, and the move let Diamond see enough thigh to appreciate Baker's hours in the gym.

"I thought you two were in love."

"Oh yeah? If you were in love, would you go kill yourself and then leave the person you been with for years money to get by for just a few months?"

99

"How much did he leave you?"

"A hundred thou. Even this house I only got for a year, then it gets turned over to some Save the Seals group. What are they going to do, put seals in the swimming pool?

"I want us both to be honest and open with each other," she said, shifting gears. Baker motioned for him to join her on the couch. He did. She slid close. The sweet scent of her perfume enveloped him.

"Do you think foul play was involved? I tried to convince the police officer there was, but he was too simple to see it."

"I don't know yet."

"Well, if there was, and it affects the will, I could be verrrrrry appreciative," she purred. Baker had penetrating pale blue eyes, and a way of nibbling her lower lip that would send most men into a tailspin. Diamond had no doubt the stylishly coiffed brown hair framing her face was hiding the high-priced work of a plastic surgeon.

Her hand touched his knee. "I love a big, strong man. Wyatt could be such a child sometimes."

She pressed her breasts against him. They felt unnaturally hard. How much of Baker was the original parts, Red wondered.

He got up and walked to the wooden deck, a Pacific-facing redwood platform that must've used up a grove of the giant trees.

"Do you have any ideas?" he asked as she followed him out.

"No," she said huskily. "Do you?"

"Was anyone here with him?"

"Not as far as I know." She leaned back against the railing next to Diamond, throwing her chest out. "Do you like the view?"

Diamond looked at the ocean. "It's nice. I could use a swim."

"Would you like to skinny dip in the pool?"

"I'd rather see Wyatt's office. And exactly where you found him."

She gave up playing the seductress, and got down to business. She told him she'd found Wyatt behind the antique mahogany desk in his office.

"He was writing out a check to some organization for juvenile delinquents."

"What did you do with the check?"

"I tore it up, of course. The estate needs every cent it can get. He wasted millions."

Diamond snooped around the office, but there wasn't much to see. Books on sociology, anthropology, and the history of rock and roll lined the shelves, with Grammies and gold records propped up between the texts.

"The cops went over the room. They took the vial of coke he'd been snorting from."

"Was anything else on his desk?"

"The usual junk. Plus this book here," she said, handing Diamond a book called *The Rocky Road: Sex and Drugs in Modern Music.*

"Can I borrow this?"

"Suit yourself."

"How did you find him?"

She walked behind the desk and sprawled across it, hands outreached. The maneuver pressed her breasts so they nearly popped from her blouse.

"Where was the checkbook? And this book?"

She put the checkbook under her chest, and the rock book in her right hand.

"Thanks," he said, taking the rock book back. He looked at its spine. There was a gap, like it had been cracked open at a certain page. He opened it and found a chapter headed, "The Good Die Young."

Baker was still sprawled provocatively across the desk.

101

"So you'll help me?" she asked.

"If I can, and it doesn't conflict with my client's interests."

She walked him to the door, pressing against him for a goodbye kiss that was more than a goodbye kiss.

"Keep in touch," she said, making "touch" sound like the kind of word written on men's-room walls.

He was glad to be out in the fresh air, away from Baker's cloying, clawing sexuality. He ankled toward the neighboring house.

If only Edwards had lived in a middle- or lower-class area, where houses were a few yards apart and people spent time on their stoop or front porch. Then Red could've counted on a neighbor seeing something. But the nearest manse was over five hundred yards away, and the view of Edwards's two-story wood shingled home was blocked by a row of neatly trimmed Monterey cypress.

Behind the cypress guardians, Diamond saw a Spanish-style villa, with tile roofs and adobe sides. He knocked at the front door. The maid answered, and he convinced her to get the master of the house after she said she'd seen and heard nothing.

A late-middle-aged man with short iron-gray hair and ramrod posture appeared. Red recognized him from bit parts in movies, where he'd played the stern police captain who inevitably ordered, "Get every man on it."

"Yes?"

"My name's Red Diamond. I'm looking into the death of your neighbor."

"Yes?"

"Did you see anyone suspicious around the Edwards house on the day he died?"

"Hah. There are always suspicious people around that

102

house. Rock-and-roll scum. Drug addicts. Pornographers. Murderers. Child molestors. Communists."

"You eyeball anyone specific? Like Joseph Stalin?"

The man ignored his remark. "The price of the whole neighborhood has gone down since those people moved in."

Diamond glanced at the complainer's home, which couldn't have cost less than five million. "Too bad."

"It is. Jews and Arabs and musicians. They're ruining a beautiful neighborhood."

"Why don't you start a petition drive to send 'em back where they came from? Especially the musicians."

"Are you being flip?"

"Perish forbid. I take it you weren't very close with Mr. Edwards?"

"Me? Socialize with those moral reprobates? I only wish he had died before he bought the house."

"You haven't answered my question about anyone over there on the day he was nice enough to die."

"The only person I saw was the woman with long blond hair. I had seen her there before. Attractive, in a cheap sort of way. She was wearing Jordache jeans and a red silk top. Some fine gold jewelry around her neck. High-heeled slingbacks."

"Wait a minute. How could you see all that?"

"I was upstairs."

"Still?"

"I just so happened to be looking through my telescope when she drove up. There's no law against that."

"Ever see Baker sunbathing?"

"Yes. She usually doesn't—wait a minute, that's got nothing to do with anything," the man said, a hint of color appearing in his cheeks.

"What kind of car was blondie driving?"

"I don't think I'll tell you."

"Maybe I'll turn up something on the people next door.

103

The police will raid them and they'll go to jail and be forced to sell the house."

"Is that really possible?"

"Anything's possible."

"It was a red Mercedes sports coupé. What will you do now?"

"Get every man on it," Diamond cracked.

Chapter Eleven

The Sheriff's Homicide Division was headquartered on the sixth floor of the Hall of Justice, in the downtown civic center.

It didn't pay to try to talk to the bulls unless you had information to swap, Red thought. But with the background he'd picked up, he might be able to trade with them. If the shinola hit the fan, it never hurt to be on talking terms with the investigating officer.

A dirty-necked cop hunting and pecking at a Royal typewriter directed Diamond to Detective Bruce Henderson. The P.I. dropped a card on Henderson's venerable desk and introduced himself. The detective managed to look bored and busy simultaneously.

"Yeah, I remember when the lines were around the block to see The Fox here," Red said, pulling up a chair.

"Who?" Henderson asked. He was powerfully built, not that tall, with eyebrows as thick as his biceps.

"The Fox. William Hickman. He kidnapped this girl, made a ransom attempt, and blew it. Wound up strangling her and then sawing her into pieces. Then he tried to pass her off as alive by wiring her eyes open."

"I think I would remember that."

At the next desk over, an old-timer had been eavesdropping. "That case was before I came on. The late twenties."

"December 1927," Diamond said. "They hung Hickman. They didn't realize Rocco had a hand in it. And the Black Dahlia case, too."

"That was LAPD's problem. Why don't you go over there and break that case for them?"

"Maybe I will. Now that I've got a snap of Rocco."

"Let's see," Henderson said.

Diamond handed over the photo of Melonie and the man's legs.

Henderson gazed at it and called out, "Charlie, see if you recognize this guy."

Charlie, the old-timer, looked at the photo and suppressed a laugh.

"I think it looks like the captain. Want to check them for dork prints?" Henderson said.

Both men guffawed and Diamond snatched the photo back. "Okay, smart alecks. I got important info on the Edwards case. You want to sit around and laugh, fine. Maybe I can get the FBI interested in it."

"Show 'em the photo of Rocco and that girl," Charlie said. "They ain't had as much excitement since they wasted Dillinger."

Diamond got up. "Thanks for nothing."

"Siddown, siddown," Henderson said. "You're awfully sensitive for a private eye that's been knocking around since the twenties."

"This is an important case. I don't have time to shoot the shit with flatfeet that don't give a damn."

"I'll make you a deal. You tell me the info you came up with, and if it leads anywhere, you go with us on it."

"Deal." Diamond took his time lighting a cigarette as the detectives watched. "Okay. I went out to the Edwards place and talked to his grieving girlfriend. She came on to me like I was Clark Gable and Tyrone Power rolled into one."

"My, what a surprise," Charlie said.

"I leave the curvy cutie with my clothes intact and go next door. It's quite a distance, but I took a shot. It paid off. The citizen there's got a telescope. He got a description of a broad who visited the premises on the day of the death."

Henderson fished around in his desk drawer.

"You lost interest or what?" Diamond asked.

"An attractive broad in a red Mercedes," Henderson said. "We didn't just fall off a truck. We know how to canvass an area."

"So who was the mystery woman?"

"No mystery. Her name is Penelope Chance. She's their producer."

"Did you grill her?"

"No, but he would've loved to," Charlie said, exchanging looks with Henderson.

"I spoke to the lady. She was out there to talk about the album they're working on. She had all kinds of paperwork to back it up. She said he had seemed a little depressed, but she was surprised he overdosed. Any more bright ideas?"

Diamond got up.

"By the way, you have a license to snoop?" Charlie asked.

"It's pending."

"While it's pending, why don't you stick to reading books about crime? It's a lot safer in the library than out in the streets."

"You ordering me off the case, copper?"

Charlie and Henderson cracked up. "You dirty rat," Charlie said. "Top of the world, Ma."

107

Muttering obscenities, Diamond stormed out of the office.

Penelope Chance was at the Valley Recording Studio. Diamond got the address and headed north on the Hollywood Freeway. It was nearing six o'clock and the roads were packed with nine-to-fivers looking forward to a hot meal and a cold beer.

The heat shimmered off thousands of look-alike sprayed stucco tract houses and garden apartment complexes as he pulled off the freeway into Sun Valley.

The fortresslike studio had architecture as inspiring as the rest of the structures in the working-class neighborhood. The windows had been bricked up, and a heavy metal door at the front was the only irregularity in the flat-yellow-painted walls. Diamond poked the intercom.

"Yeah?"

"Is Penelope Chance there?"

"Who wants to know?"

"Red Diamond."

"Wait."

After a minute or so, the door buzzed and Diamond pulled it open. A haggard man in a Rolling Stones T-shirt greeted him with an emotionless, "Follow me."

Diamond trailed him down a hall lined with posters of Fleetwood Mac, the Beach Boys, the Eagles, Linda Ronstadt, and dozens of other names that meant nothing to the P.I. Most of the posters were autographed.

The haggard man pointed to a door with a sign STUDIO B: SHUT UP OR STAY OUT. Diamond knocked and entered without waiting for an answer.

It was dark in the small room, with a dim overhead light and hundreds of glowing meters. A man in his mid-thirties—whose long dark hair, ascetic features, and trimmed beard made him look like Christ—sat at the mammoth console, watching forty-two numbered meters and indicator lights and nimbly adjusting a field of switches.

A woman sat next to the man. She was intently gazing at something on the other side of a glass panel. Red couldn't see her face, or what it was that was holding her attention.

The bearded man looked at Diamond and shouted, "Who the fuck are you?"

Yelling was the only way to be heard, since four gargantuan Altec speakers were blasting out singing louder than Ethel Merman with a bullhorn.

"That's okay, Cliff. I spoke to Sharkey this morning. Mr. Diamond is here to see me," the woman said. He still couldn't see her face.

She had a perfect hourglass figure and blond hair tied up in a loose bun. She sat in a languid slouch that showed she was used to being looked at.

"Cliff's the best engineer in the business," she said, trying to make peace. "Mr. Diamond's a private investigator looking into Wyatt's death."

Cliff lowered the volume on the monitor speakers. "He was a decent fellow, not like most string players," Cliff said, his fingers continuing to tinker with the switches as the meters danced. "String players are prima donnas. Drummers are wild, do too many drugs. Lead singers are degenerates and egomaniacs."

"I know, the only good people in a studio are the engineers," Chance said. "Right?"

"Some of the producers are okay," Cliff said grudgingly. "You want me to boost the low or up the harmonizer?"

"Both," Chance said, as Cliff's fingers hopped from fader levers to an illuminated slide switch. "Peter needs all the help he can get."

Diamond stepped into the room. He could see the singer on the other side of the window.

109

"Who's that?" Diamond asked.

"Peter Piper. I suppose you'll want to talk to him?"

"Yes."

"After the session. It's going badly enough without you getting him worked up."

Seated atop a padded bar stool, Piper's feet barely touched the ground. He was handsome, in a pixieish sort of way. Red wondered if his ears were pointed under his long black hair.

"Ted Kirk warned me about you," Chance said. "I hope you don't have too many tough questions." She sounded more amused than intimidated. "What do you want to know?"

"Who killed Wyatt Edwards?"

"The police are calling it an accident."

"Those bozos wouldn't know a killer if he hit them on the nose. They're missing the ball."

"In what way?"

"I don't know yet. What were you doing at the Edwards place?"

"Arranging a time for him to come into the studio."

"When it was convenient for the three of them?"

"No. They come in separately and work with the studio musicians. Peter laid down a scratch vocal, Wynn the drum work, and Wyatt had done most of his basic tracks. Now Peter has to do the overdub and hopefully we can smooth things out in the master mix. I'm counting on Cliff to save my ass."

Cliff grunted.

"Isn't it easier to do it together?" Diamond asked.

"Not when they hate each other."

"Do they?"

"Maybe hate's too strong a word. Despise."

"Why?"

"They're spoiled children with too much money and too little self-control."

Penelope spoke into a hand mike. "Peter, honey, that didn't quite work. Let's try it again."

"I can't. I can't do it anymore. I've been at it for hours."

"Peter, please," she said. "One more time. Think of your fans out there waiting for this album. We're already a week past our deadline."

Piper twisted his lips in a long-suffering pout.

"Fuckin' jerk-off," Cliff mumbled.

She let her hand off the mike switch. "Careful or he'll throw a full-blown tantrum."

"What are you talking about?" Piper asked, peering at them through the glass.

She clicked down the mike. "How great it's going up to now. It would be a pity to stop."

"Who's that in there with you?" Piper asked, looking at Diamond.

"He's just a friend," she lied. "Let's get back to work."

Piper resumed singing after a bit more coaxing.

"Why was Edwards depressed?" Diamond asked.

"His sessions hadn't gone very well."

"What about the book in his hand?"

"We'll have to continue our chat another time," she said, turning to face him. "I really must—what's the matter?"

Diamond's mouth had dropped open as he recognized Penelope Chance. The heart-shaped face, full lush lips, a pert nose, eyes that sparkled like diamonds.

"Fifi!" Diamond gasped.

"Who?"

"Fifi, it's Red."

Confused, she turned back to the console. "Okay, Red, we'll talk later."

"But, Fifi—"

"No buts. I don't have time for this. I've got work to do here. The A & R bitch from Vine-L calls me every fifteen

111

minutes, the studio costs two hundred an hour, and Cliff costs nearly as much. Not that he isn't worth it," she said, patting the engineer.

It was a signal. She couldn't talk with the mug next to her. Red contemplated knocking him out, but decided against it. More of Rocco's heavies could be watching.

"I'll meet you at Sonny Brown's. It's a bar over on Laurel Canyon Boulevard. In less than an hour."

"Maybe I should wait here with you?"

"No," she said firmly. "Things will go much quicker if you don't hang around. Believe me."

He left, stopping off at a florist and a candy shop, then went back and sat in his car in the parking lot, watching the studio. He waited to make sure she got out of there safely.

"Ohhhh, Red, you're such an animal," my doll sighed as she took a drag on my cigarette. Her hair was soft as the inside of a down pillow as I ran my hand through it. Our hearts were thumping in harmony, as Gene Krupa and Anita O'Day worked their magic on the radio.

"What's going to happen?" she asked me in that throaty voice that a guy could mistake for Lauren Bacall's.

"Whatever you want," I said, cupping one of her golden globes.

"Ohhhhh, Red," she said. "I mean, in the future."

"More of the same."

"What about Rocco? What if he lives?"

"I plugged him good, cupcake. By now he should be at the gates of hell."

"But, Red, didn't I tell you about the bulletproof vest he's been wearing?"

I sat up abruptly. "No."

"Oh, I'm sorry. I guess I forgot."

"Don't sweat it, sweetheart. It's not your fault."

112

*She was crying. "What trouble I've been for you, Red. I
would understand if you never wanted to see me again."*

So I had to reassure her.

I was getting pretty winded.

*"You know I ain't running out on you, my little chick-
adee," I said, doing a W.C. Fields impression that wouldn'ta
fooled a deaf man.*

"You're wonderful. But I'm so worried."

"Don't be."

"What if Rocco comes after us again?"

"Maybe he didn't make it anyway."

*I had spoken too soon. The door to the room crashed
open. Rocco and two gun-toting hoods barged in.*

*With a rod pointed at my sweetie, I had to let the goons
put the handcuffs on me. They wouldn't let me put nothing
else on. They liked that. They liked pawing Fifi even more.*

*They tied me to a heavy wooden chair. I struggled and
Rocco laughed.*

*A dumpy hoople in a white smock walked in like he
expected trumpets to announce his arrival.*

*"Vell, vat have ve here?" he asked, looking at Fifi so
long his wire-rim glasses steamed up.*

"Do your tricks, doc," Rocco said.

*They tied my baby down, the ropes biting cruelly into
the tender pink flesh.*

*The Kraut doctor took out a pocket watch on a gold
chain. "Dim the lights," he ordered, and one of the goons
did.*

*"Vatch the vatch," he said, setting it in motion a foot
away from her face.*

"No."

"You tell the creep, sugar," I piped up.

*A goon rewarded me with a pistol whip across my ear.
He pressed the gun into my temple.*

"Do what the doc says," Rocco sneered, "or loverboy here gets ventilated."

"Don't do it, Fifi," I told her, but it was no use.

"You are growing sleepy, sleepy," the Kraut said in a voice as slimy as a toad's belly.

Her eyes drooped.

"Wake up," I yelled.

The strongarms hit me to get my attention, then shoved a gag in my mouth. The hoople in white began his mesmerism act again. Soon my doll was in a trance.

"Now we can have some fun," Rocco said.

One of the goons was drooling as they undid her bonds.

"Do you mind telling me what you're talking about?" Penelope asked as they sat in the darkened bar. "I mean, the roses are nice. So are the chocolates. But this story about Fifi and Rocco?"

"You don't have to play it close to the vest, sugar," Diamond said. "I'd know you anywhere. The innocent baby blues that don't seem to go with the lush, sensuous mouth. The long, firm neck that cries out to be nibbled, the tender flesh of the shoulders leading to the—"

"Okay, enough of an anatomy lesson. It's really flattering, except I've never seen you before in my life."

"It's posthypnotic suggestion. Don Diavolo taught me about it when I caught his magic act in Greenwich Village. Rocco had that quack do it to you after that time in the motel. Don't you remember?"

She sipped her Tom Collins and sniffed one of the roses.

"You disappeared. I've been searching all over for you. Rocco has too. But I got to you first," the P.I. said gleefully. "Do you remember any of it?"

Amused and confused, she chewed a candy and studied him.

"Of course you can't," Diamond said. "That's what

makes it so tricky. But we'll get it straightened out. Don't you worry."

"You say I'm the woman you've been looking for since when?"

"Right after Prohibition."

"Do you take a lot of drugs?"

"Never touch them. Unless you count the time Rocco injected me with opium in Singapore."

"If I'm your long-lost girl, you'll do what I say? Obey me completely? And let me know exactly what you're up to?"

"A dick's gotta have loyalty to his clients."

"Of course. But your number-one priority is catching this Rocco Rico. And I'm your best shot at finding him, right?"

Diamond nodded.

"Then you should let me know everything first. Maybe it will help jog my memory back."

He knew it was Fifi for sure. What other dame could think so clearly, even with an insane killer on her trail?

"We'll keep our arrangement quiet," she said. "It will help keep me safe from Rocco. Agreed?"

"How about we seal the deal with a kiss?"

She slid over next to him in the booth and he put a lip lock on her. Fifi was a bit rusty. It wasn't the way he remembered it. But maybe she was being reserved because they were in a public place. Or maybe it was the hypnosis.

"Is there anything else you've learned about Peter and the Pickled Peppers that you might want to tell your Fifi?" she asked.

"Like what?"

"I don't know. You're the investigator."

"It's still early in the caper, cupcake."

Chapter Twelve

He showed Fifi the photo of Melonie and Rocco. No dice. Red was concerned she didn't recognize Rocco's legs right away. He didn't want to push things—it was like waking a sleepwalker.

"Tell me about the group," Diamond said as he started on his third bourbon. Fifi nursed her Tom Collins.

"What's to say? I've been doing a lot of thinking about them since Edwards died. He had talent. He was frequently compared to Eric Clapton."

Fifi had been talking somberly. "I cried enough. Wallowing doesn't help anybody. You want to know their background? The three of them met in San Francisco. They started playing gigs in that Jefferson Airplane–Grateful Dead circle. They nearly were a featured act at Altamont. Edwards did some studio work, so did Wynn. Piper's got more personality than talent, but he kept them together. Every now and then one gets in trouble so they wind up back in the headlines."

"Why stick with them?"

"It was the only way to get ahead in rock. I've been around the scene since I was sixteen. With a sore throat I can outsing Piper."

116

"I remember you always were musically inclined. That time on the Champs Elysées you knocked 'em dead."

She stared at him, perplexed.

"You had to keep the Nazis entertained while the Free French and me was setting up the explosives. You sang 'See What the Boys in the Back Room Will Have.' That ammo-dump explosion was music to our ears."

"Oh, sure, that time," she said. "Anyway, I got a meeting to go to."

"Why do you stay with these bums? You got talent."

"When I was ready, girl-groups were a novelty act. They didn't want serious female performers. Now, there's a better chance, but I'm too old."

"Too old. You look just like the first time I saw you, at the Trocadero when Eddie and Al LeBaron owned it. You was working at the RKO Studio."

"What year was that?" she challenged.

"A few years ago. Let's see, Eddie sold the joint about 1944 when he went off to fight in the Big One. I guess 1943."

Fifi finished her drink. "I better go."

"I'll come along, make sure you're okay."

"No. I'm going to a woman's group."

"Sounds like fun."

"The Dianas is women only."

"Why?"

"It's for networking."

"What?"

"We're trying to establish an old-girl network, like men have used to shut us out."

"What about Rocco?"

"What about him?"

"You need protection."

"Red, I've gotten along fine without a bodyguard all these years. If anything, you and I together will attract his

117

attention. Besides, don't you need to go off and tilt at windmills?"

"Windmills? Are you talking about that time in Holland, when the spies were headquartered in—"

"Another time. I'm going to be late." She got up.

"When will I see you again?"

"You want to interview Peter?"

"Definitely."

"I'll set something up for you tomorrow. About eleven," she said, reciting an address on Tigertail Road in Brentwood.

"Will you be there?"

"Probably not," she said. "But let me know how it goes."

He gave her a goodbye peck and she was off. He settled the tab and followed her.

Sometimes that dame could be too cocky for her own good, Red thought as she got in her red Mercedes-Benz sports coupé. He would keep an eye on her, from a discreet distance.

Fifi stayed on city streets, heading west and then south into Sherman Oaks. The coupé climbed into the hills, with Diamond hanging behind. She turned off Beverly Glen near the Stone Canyon reservoir, then onto a small private road. She came to a high metal gate, announced her name into a speaker and the gate swung open. An eight-foot stone wall ringed a multiacre estate.

Inside, Diamond could make out well-lit gardens with statues of muscular women grasping bows and arrows. Sprinklers hissed on perfect green lawns. He couldn't see the house, but a Rolls-Royce, Jaguar, and Mercedes-Benz were visible in the circular driveway.

He parked his car up the road a bit and watched. Two more luxury cars, with female drivers, zipped by and were allowed in. The traffic stopped, and he was alone with the crickets and the night smells of jasmine and honeysuckle.

* * *

"Vat do you plan to do vit her?" the hypnotist asked as Rocco's slobbering goons untied her.

"She doesn't want me, so everybody's going to have her. But I get her first," Rocco said with a chuckle. "I got a club down by the docks. She's gonna be the featured attraction. If there's anything left after me and the boys get through with her. You like that, Red?"

I growled pure hate through the gag.

"Vat about me?"

"You get a turn too," Rocco said. "Can anything get her out of the trance?"

"She is completely under my vill," the mesmerist said. "But it is best to let the psyche settle down into the proper levels of consciousness. It vill take no more zen ten minutes."

"I gotta talk to Torchy about burning down that orphanage. Leave the shamus alone with her. He can think about all the fun he's gonna be missing. You like that, peeper?"

He ripped the gag from my mouth and I unloaded a string of obscenities to make a teamster blush. I bucked and struggled, but it was no use. The stainless-steel cuffs tore at my wrists, the rope held me flat against the chair.

They walked out laughing, leaving me naked as a jaybird and helpless, with my Fifi in a trance only a few feet away.

The idea of what Rocco had in mind for her was driving me crazy. Which is what Rocco wanted. This was worse than a dozen strongarms with crowbars making like Lionel Hampton on my kneecaps.

"Fifi! Fifi! Fifi!" I yelled, but she continued to stare at me with unseeing eyes.

It was as close as I ever been to giving up, throwing in the towel, and admitting that Rocco had beaten me. If it wasn't for the fate worse than death that awaited Fifi, I mighta done it. But I couldn't let that happen to my doll.

119

I stopped relying on my muscles and put my gray matter to work. How could I get her out of the hypnotic state?

I tried the cuffs again. Then it hit me.

I wiggled the cuffs and they caught the light from the lamp. I moved my wrists until the reflection bounced off the baby blues I loved to lose myself in.

"Fi-fi, Fi-fi," I said slowly. "Listen to me. You are Fifi La Roche. You have a will of your own. Do you understand?"

Nothing. I repeated it I don't now how many times, with as much authority as I could muster. I knew the door might open at any second, and the goon squad return. But I couldn't fail. It was high-stakes poker, with our lives as the ante.

"Fi-fi, Fi-fi, this is Red. Pull yourself together. We don't have much time."

Right before the door opened, I thought I saw her blink.

It was past midnight when the cars rolled out of the estate. Fifi's was the fourth to leave, and Diamond slipped into the procession easily. He tailed her to Santa Monica, to a house a block up from the ocean.

The building was painted an ugly green. It had a sloping roof, elaborate gables, and about a quarter-acre of land. Anywhere else it might've gone for eighty thou. In Southern California, it was worth a half-million.

Diamond saw her go in and turn on the lights. He circled the block once to make sure no wiseguys were staking the place out. The coast was clear, and he called it a night.

He was up early the next morning to catch Wynn as he made his morning run. He met him on San Vicente. Red timed it so he was still fresh, as Wynn was breathing hard.

"Have you solved the case yet?" Wynn asked sarcastically as they loped along.

"Soon."

"I think people smart enough to get away with murder should be allowed to do it."

"If they get away with it, then they do," Diamond said.

"True enough. Have you read any Nietzsche?"

"I think I had some of his nuts once."

Wynn did a double take and pondered the response. "That's lichee. Lichee nuts."

"Yeah."

"Nietzsche talked about man and superman, how there are those born to greatness. Like me."

"I think you're too modest," the P.I. said.

"Power is meant to be seized. Like groupies. Is it my job to throw a thirteen-year-old out of my bed? No. If society puts her there, I say why not enjoy it?"

Diamond reached into his pocket and produced the photo of Melonie and Rocco. "You recognize the girl or the guy?"

"She is so typical. Maybe. Him, I can tell he does not stay in shape. Look how flabby his thighs are."

"What about threats?" Diamond asked, taking the picture back. "Did the group or Edwards get any threats recently?"

"We always get threats. Either the fans think they are God, or we are God, or we owe them money, or they just want to get their names in the paper. They are disgusting little people . . ."

"Who buy your records," Diamond said. "Any new faces around Edwards that he would've trusted enough to let in his house?"

"No. Well, he did talk about meeting this woman he knew from the old days. She was down on her luck, and he was going to help her out. He was always doing that. He liked taking care of stray dogs, bums, cripples," Wynn

121

said contemptuously. "Hard times are coming. We need hard men to rule them. Are you prepared?"

"For what?"

"The apocalypse. I have enough food and water to last six months. Firepower to hold off an army of beggars. I might let you share my future. I will need a bodyguard."

"If that's the future, I'll stick with the past."

"It's your life. If you want to die with the masses, fine. Me, I want to live forever."

Wynn speeded up as a burst of adrenalin kicked his system into overdrive. He was soon a block ahead of Diamond, who wondered how much more claptrap he could listen to before knocking Wynn on his fascist fanny. He reminded Red of Father Coughlin, mixing philosophy and hate to suit his own beliefs.

Wynn was crossing the street as the yellow Mack truck zoomed forward against a red light. The drummer was squashed flat against the front of the vehicle.

It happened so fast, Wynn didn't even have a chance to cry out. He was as lifeless as a brewer's-yeast flapjack. The truck, which had no license plates, was roaring away. Diamond's gun was out, but too many cars were blocking a clean shot.

By the time the cops were done questioning him, it was noon. Diamond called Piper, who remained petulant even after the P.I. told him why he was going to be late.

On fifteen acres of prime land, Piper had a horseback-riding trail, helipad, stables, pool and sauna, a maze made from trimmed hedges, and a tennis court. Piper was playing tennis when Diamond was admitted to the estate.

The pro was a lanky Scandinavian who was doing his best to lob the ball so that Piper could hit it.

"That's it. Enough," Piper shouted, spotting Diamond. "Beat it, Lars. I've had enough."

Lars nodded and walked away.

"You were supposed to be here at eleven," Piper said as Diamond approached him.

"I told you, Wynn got killed by a hit-and-run and I had to give the coppers a statement."

"Not much of a loss to humanity," Piper said and sat under an umbrella at a round table. He pushed a button twice.

The rock singer's custom-tailored tennis whites were dripping wet. He was panting like a greyhound after a race, and was about as skinny. His small features added to his pixieish look.

Piper had let the silence hang in the air as he unabashedly studied Diamond.

"Not very impressive," he said, looking down his nose at the P.I.

"You do fashion commentary when you're not making like Johnny Mercer?"

"Who's he?" Piper asked.

A well-stacked maid in a classic black-and-white outfit brought out a pitcher full of clear liquid and a highball glass. Piper goosed her. She jumped dutifully, but Red had the feeling she expected it.

"You didn't do very well at protecting Charlie, did you?" Piper asked, sipping the drink.

"I wasn't hired to do that. If I was, it wouldn't have happened."

"Oh yeah, how could you protect him?"

"First thing, I wouldn'ta let him follow the same route every day. Makes it too easy for anyone wants to whack him."

"You've done a lot of bodyguard work?"

"Enough. I don't like it."

"Why?"

"Celebrities, politicians, the kind of people you guard are pains in the ass. Used to getting their way. If I told

123

Charlie to do something and he didn't, I'd have to quit. It's my rep on the line if he gets plugged."

"I'm a celebrity."

"I know."

"I don't believe I like your manners."

"When you make up your mind, let me know."

They sat in silence. Diamond lit a cigarette while Piper sipped.

"Tell me more about being a bodyguard," Piper said.

"What's to tell? People think it's exciting, mixing and mingling with the big shots. But you don't sit and talk with Barbara Hutton, you got to keep an eye on everyone but the person you're guarding, watching for the sudden move, the hand in the pocket. You got to ignore the plunging necklines, the dolls in swimsuits coming on because they know you're a man's man."

"That would be the hardest part of the job for me."

"You gonna offer me a drink?"

"Babette didn't bring another glass."

Diamond hoisted the pitcher and took a swallow. It was a tart gin-and-tonic mixture that felt good going down. "No problem."

"I like your style," Piper said. "Or lack of it."

"I ain't here to be stylish. I'm here to keep you from getting killed."

"You think someone will try?"

"Probably."

"Just because Wynn got run over."

"It was deliberate. I got my suspicions about Wyatt Edwards's death."

"Will you protect me?" Piper asked, with the barest hint of tremor in his voice.

"You want to hire a houseboy with a gun, you better get another boy. I don't put up with crap from clients."

"I'll pay whatever your fee is. Double that."

124

"The money ain't the problem. I got a client already. Two clients. But let me see what Fifi says."

"Fifi?"

"You know her under another name. Penelope."

"That dyke."

Diamond slapped him across the face. "You don't talk that way about her or you'll be eating with a straw for months."

Piper sprang up. "How dare you, how dare you strike me! You're fired!"

"You can't fire me. I never took the job."

He drove back to his place on Fountain Avenue, exercised to burn off his aggravation, showered, and curled up with the book that Edwards had been reading when he died.

The names of the groups didn't mean anything to Diamond. The Strawberry Alarm Clock, Blue Cheer, Herman's Hermits, Sam the Sham and the Pharaohs, the Ronettes, Righteous Brothers, Moody Blues, Canned Heat, Pink Floyd, Led Zeppelin, Iron Butterfly.

The author, Alan Sonnenschein, had outlined the history of rock and roll and how the sexual revolution and the boom in drug abuse had paralleled its rise.

Diamond put Peter and the Pickled Peppers album on his turntable. He poured himself a beer and listened. There was a lot of singing, a lot of guitar playing, and a lot of drumming. It sounded like a lot of noise.

The album cover had a photo of a woman wearing a mink coat, with nothing underneath, kissing a car muffler.

He scrutinized the jacket notes. The songs spanned a period of twenty years. "Love Me and My Car" was the earliest, from a 1967 album. "Party All Night" was recorded last year. In between, they had done songs like "Gimme Your Bod" (1968), "Kill For Peace" (1970), "The

Grass is Growin'" (1973), "Dead Dolphin Blues" (1977), and "It's Mine" (1980).

The side ended. He flipped it over and went back to reading Sonnenschein's book. He was up to the part Edwards had been at when he died.

The chapter included profiles of various dead musicians. None lived past their forties, and virtually every major group was touched by the Grim Reaper.

Brian Jones, drowned while using drugs; Bobby Darin, heart attack; Jimi Hendrix, choked on vomit while under the influence of drugs; Janis Joplin, heroin overdose; Jim Croce, plane crash; Buddy Holly, plane crash; Marvin Gaye, shot; Sid Vicious, heroin overdose; Keith Moon, downer overdose; Jim Morrison, unknown; Elvis Presley, heart attack; Otis Redding, plane crash. And on and on.

Sonnenschein explained that musicians traveled frequently by small plane. The more time in the air, the more chances of coming down hard. Drugs and fast living had always been an occupational hazard for entertainers.

Why would Edwards have been groping for that chapter? Was he trying to get his own place in history? Looking for others who had gone before him? Could it be a coincidence?

The P.I. listened to the Peter and the Pickled Peppers album again. It was a dirty job, but somebody had to do it.

Chapter Thirteen

Fifi called early the next morning. She spent a few sentences on how sad Wynn's death was, but Red had the feeling she would've been more busted up over a two-handkerchief movie.

"Life is tough, angel," he said. "Wynn talked about survival of the fittest. I guess he couldn't cut the mustard."

"I heard you didn't get along too well with Peter," she said.

"That's safe to say. Why don't you come over and we can perk coffee together?"

"I have to go meet with Kirk and Peter, then to the studio. We have most of the tracks down from Wyatt and Charlie, and we can probably get studio musicians to sweeten it. But it's still a headache."

"I'll tag along."

"Better not. If Peter sees you, he'll throw a temper tantrum. Why don't we get together tonight? Say seven?"

"I'll be holding my breath till then."

"Had a good time, shamus?" Rocco sneered.

"Not as good as I'd have wringing your rotten neck."

"Crack wise all you want. The party's about to begin," Rocco said.

There was a knock at the door and a third gunsel came in. After taking in an eyeful of my baby he said, "Mr. Rico, there's a phone call."

"Business before pleasure," Rocco said. He turned to his goons. "You can play with her, but no serious stuff. That's for me."

He left and the goon with the leaky puss hurried to my honey. She stood stiffly in his apelike arms.

"Get your paws off her," I rumbled.

He did at first, then realized my predicament. He smirked and re-embraced Fifi.

"Make her do, you know, things," the goon said to the hypnotist.

"Only if I'm next," the bum said.

"I'll get you all, if I have to go to hell to do it," I said.

The hypnotist stepped up close to Fifi. "My vill is your vill. You are alone with your boyfriend, Mr. Red Diamond. You have been apart a long time. You give him a big kiss."

"I'll kill you, I'll kill you," I yelled, bucking and kicking like a bronco with a too-tight saddle.

She softened and put her arms around the hoodlum. Her hands went up and down him in a steamy embrace that was meant for me. I was yelling so loud, nobody but Fifi could concentrate.

"Gag him," the hypnotist ordered, and the goon waiting for thirds came over. He put his hand near my mouth, and I bit down like his finger was a crunchy carrot and I was Bugs Bunny. I held on as he smacked my head.

The other two creeps turned to see what happened. Before I could say, "What's up, doc?" Fifi had boosted the goon's gun and was aiming it at his breadbasket.

"Hey," he said and he swiped at her.

She let him have it. He dropped to the floor like a lump of lard. The other goon wasn't going anywhere with my choppers anchored to his finger. The hypnotist sniveled.

"You're bad, bad men," Fifi said, keeping the gun on

the others while fishing the cuff keys from their fallen companion's pocket.

She made the bloody-fingered goon undo the cuffs.

"I ain't had my rabies shots either," I told him as I put him out of his misery with a solid hook to the chin.

The hypnotist was crying for mercy. I only hit him once, but I hear they used more wire to put his jaw back together than they did on the Brooklyn Bridge.

"Oh Red, you're wonderful," Fifi said as I took the roscoe out of her sweet hands.

"You ain't too shabby yourself, doll."

"But how will we get out of here?"

I lifted the second gun from the downed strongarm.

"Gimme a minute or two and I'll think of something. You better put clothes on so I can get my mind offa making whoopee."

She tittered. No one titters like my baby.

I couldn't help but watch her get dressed. It was my favorite sight, except in reverse.

It gave me an idea. Actually, it gave me lots of ideas. But one of them would help us get out of there so we could go back to my place and see about all those other ideas.

Red took his remaining copies of the Polaroid of Melonie and Rocco and headed out to the beach to see what Ross had turned up.

Rolling Ross's stand wasn't opened, although the sign said it should've been. Diamond went to a nearby hot dog stand. The petite brunette at the counter had a perfect tan and white teeth that gleamed as she smiled. She smiled easily.

"Ross usually late to open?" Diamond asked.

"Never," she said.

"This the first time it happened?"

"Yes. I wonder if he's sick?" she said, as if the idea had just occurred to her.

"You know where he lives?"

She shook her head. "Maybe the boss knows. He rents the space to him."

The boss's name was Stanley Mason, and he operated out of a crowded real-estate office on Washington Boulevard. He had a bottle of Maalox and lots of chewed pencils on his desk.

"No way I can give it to you," Mason said. "Invasion of privacy. Everybody sues. Too many lawyers. Mothers sue kids, girlfriends sue boyfriends, brothers sue each other. Don't talk to me about partners."

"Too many lawyers."

"That's for sure. I got more lawyers than a dog's got fleas. To tell the truth, I'd rather have the fleas."

Mason continued to rant about deadbeat tenants who destroyed property, greedy politicians who hustled campaign donations and then forgot their contributors, and assorted bureaucrats, tax collectors, and inspectors.

"Maybe you can do me a favor," Diamond said, after nodding along agreeably for a few minutes.

"As long as it won't get me hauled into court. I'm getting so I know the clerks on a first-name basis."

"Could you call Ross at home and tell him his buddy Red Diamond is here?"

Mason thought for a minute. "I guess that couldn't cause me any extra trouble."

Mason checked an index card and dialed. "No answer," he said after a dozen rings."

"Why don't you let me have his address and I'll go check it out?"

"He's a good tenant," Mason mused. "Responsible."

"How about it?"

"I can't do it, pal, much as I'd like to."

"Let's say you had to go to the can and someone were to look in your files and find the address. You wouldn't take the rap."

130

Mason picked up a pencil and chomped the end. "Okay. Now that you mention it, I do have to go."

"Thanks."

"For what?" Mason asked as he got up.

"For talking to me."

Diamond glanced at Ross's card and headed over to the skate merchant's home on Sherman Canal Court.

Venice had been planned as a California knock-off of the city with the same name in Italy. The developer had built canals, bridges, and quaint houses. In some spots, it still looked a little like Gondola-town.

But the hard light of day showed garbage floating with the ducks in the canals, decaying buildings, and the handiwork of speculators who dumped helpless old people out of their homes.

A Volkswagen that had been hit more times than Max Schmeling was parked in the dirt driveway of Ross's bungalow. Another VW, even older and more beat-up, was parked in the front yard. Grass and flowers had grown as high as the fender. A gang of ducks were sitting next to the front stairs. They quacked like fowl watchdogs when Diamond walked up and rapped out a tune on the weathered wooden door.

No answer. Diamond tried the knob. It turned and he stepped in. The smell hit him. He drew his gun. He knew what he'd find. It was only a matter of where he'd find it.

In the bedroom, lying in a heap near the dresser, was a partially clothed Ross. He had a bullet hole in the middle of his forehead, a grizzly red-rimmed third eye. The flies had discovered the corpse.

Red shooed them away, though he knew he couldn't win. He balled his fists and longed for someone to hit.

He searched the house, learning only that Ross was a sloppy housekeeper with a limited wardrobe. In the front room, where Ross had a fish tank, a TV, and a worn recliner, Diamond found the ledgers from Edwards's charities and jotted the names down on a piece of paper.

The ducks quacked. He tiptoed forward, gun in hand.

The door creaked. Diamond swung it open and planted a fist in the intruder's stomach. The P.I. chopped down on the back of the man's head and he fell onto the frayed Indian rug. Diamond slammed the door and aimed his .38.

"Roll over real slow, dirtbag. Move too quick and I use your spine for target practice."

The man rolled over.

"Hi, Dad."

Chapter Fourteen

"What the hell are you doing here?" Diamond demanded after he saw that Sean was okay. "No, don't tell me now. We better get out of here."

"What's that terrible smell?"

"The reason we better get out of here. Ross is dead."

"Wow! Did you kill him, too?"

"No, I didn't kill him," Diamond snapped. "Let's get a move on. Can you travel?"

They rendezvoused at Diamond's apartment.

"I was going to call you with the long-distance numbers I came up with, then I figured you might need a hand," Sean explained.

"Red Diamond don't need a hand from nobody. Least of all an amateur. I hear about these cutesy old English ladies solving cases over tea and crumpets. Horsecrap. It takes a pro."

"Well, maybe I can learn from you. It's sort of like a practical psychology course."

"I don't have time to play wet nurse, kid. Three people have cashed in their chips on this case." Diamond recited the facts to Sean, hoping to scare him back to college. The youth sat listening, open-mouthed and attentive.

"Fascinating," he said when Diamond was done. "Who did it?"

"I don't know. Yet. I got a question for you. How'd you wind up at Ross's?"

"There was no one at your office when I stopped by, so I decided to do a little snooping on my own. I called some of the phone numbers from our bills and went to see the people. Most were girls who were sort of . . . loose."

"I'm shocked."

"One of the women, she goes by the name of Busty Betsy, said that I wasn't the first to be asking about Melonie, and she told me about Ross."

"And Melonie?"

"She thought she'd seen her but she wasn't sure."

"Had anyone else been around asking about Melonie?"

"Darn. I forgot to ask."

"Okay, let's go back and talk to her."

"Uh, you don't need to. I'll go there."

"You think Red Diamond's gonna miss a chance to meet a broad named Busty Betsy?"

Over Sean's protests, they drove to Betsy's house in the southern part of Hollywood.

Wood-frame houses that were attractive and new when the talkies first moved to Los Angeles were set out on small lots. Betsy's house was better kept than most. The white clapboard siding, shutters, and trim were freshly painted. She was polishing her classic 1965 Mustang. It had vanity plates reading TRY ME and a MALES WANTED: APPLY WITHIN bumpersticker.

Betsy was a chunky redhead with meaty thighs that burst out from cut-off shorts. Her age was approaching her breast size, and her breasts were approaching her waist. As she moved, they made like pom-pom guns under a T-shirt that said FOR A GOOD TIME, CALL.

"Like what you see?" she asked, looking up. She recognized Sean. "Oh, you're back. Want to go at it again, or you just showing your friend the best there is?"

Sean turned redder than a sunburnt albino and stammered.

"He's shy, ain't that cute," Betsy said to Diamond. "You don't look like the shy type. For fifty bucks, you can have an experience you'll never forget."

"I'll give you one you won't forget for free. You're under arrest."

"What?"

"You been around long enough to know better than to proposition a detective. And to take advantage of junior here."

"Take advantage? The dumb cluck damn near broke my neck with his bouncing up and down. He needs a trampoline, not a waterbed."

"I . . . I was . . ." Sean began.

"Can it, kid," Diamond said. "What you did is your business."

"Why do you always pick on the women? How about locking him up as a john?" she asked.

"I would've, only he gave me the information I needed."

"What kind of information?"

"Confidential."

"I know more than he does. He didn't even know—"

"Okay, let's you and me go in and talk. Kid, wait in the car."

He followed her into the house. She put her hands on her hips challengingly. "What do you want, half and half, around the world, or straight up and down?"

"I told you, information."

"I never met a cop who would turn down free action."

"You just met one. I want to know about Ross. And Melonie."

135

"The girl in the photo?"

Diamond held out his picture of Rocco's legs and Melonie. "Hold on," Betsy said, and she got her glasses out of a small wooden table.

"Boy, this john is hairy."

"You know him?"

"I know a lot of hairy guys."

"This one's name is Rocco."

"Most of the tricks don't give their names. If they do, they're named John or Joe or something else white bread."

"He's used lots of aliases. What about Melonie?"

"She don't look that much like the girl in that kid's photo, but I guess it is," she said squinting. "I don't know her."

"We're going downtown," Diamond barked.

"What? I been level with you."

"Bull. You forgot your phone number turned up in the girl's bill."

Betsy was quiet for a moment. "Okay, okay. She called me asking about work. I said I'd put her in touch with some people when she came out here. I got her a booking at a party."

"What party?"

"I don't remember the name, but it was in a funny-shaped building. It was a record company, and the building was like a doughnut."

Diamond nodded. "Vine-L Records. We've been watching them."

He stared into Betsy's face, letting the silence hang in the air like an ugly storm cloud.

"Is that it?" she asked. "Do you drop the beef?"

"One last question and I forget I ever saw you. Has anyone else been by asking about the girl?"

"Sure, Rossie. He's a sweetie. Helped set up the day-care center where I got my kid. I told him."

"Anybody else?"

He saw the fear flicker across her eyes as she shook her head.

"Betsy, don't blow it."

"No one, no one, I swear."

"I'll give you time to think it over."

"That's it?"

"That's it," he said. "For now."

"You see, I was asking her questions and she said maybe if we got friendly she'd remember and we went—"

"Don't sweat it, kid."

"How'd it go in there, uh, I mean you weren't in there that long, uh, did you, uh, get anything, uh . . ."

"You're gonna trip on your tongue if you don't come up for air," Diamond said. "I asked her a slew of questions and she gave me a slew of answers. She was telling the truth most of the time."

"Speaking of telling the truth, you impersonated a police officer. Isn't that a crime?"

"I didn't impersonate nobody. I told her I was a detective, which I am. I threatened her with arrest, which is a power every citizen has. Maybe you and her jumped to the wrong conclusions."

"You misled her."

"Life is tough."

"Where are we going now?"

"You want to help out?"

"Sure," Sean said enthusiastically.

"I got a hunch about this thing. I want you to go to the main library and check out the dates and locations where rock stars died. Look for a pattern."

"That could take days."

"The dull legwork is what usually cracks the case

137

wide open," Diamond said. "Of course, if you don't want to help . . ."

"No, I want to. But how is this connected with Melonie?"

"She was traveling in these circles. I got a feeling it ties in."

"Hunches are often based on logic that stems from subconscious clues and can't be verbalized," Sean said knowingly. "A lot of paranormal phenomena can be traced to the same level of consciousness."

"That's what I always say."

Diamond dropped Sean by his car and drove to Vine-L Records. As he pulled into the lot, he saw Fifi's red coupé. He raced up the stairs. Could his doll be trapped in the middle of a sex orgy?

"You can't go in. Mr. Kirk's in the middle of a meeting," the cold-blooded secretary said.

"Tell him Red Diamond wants to talk to him."

"He's got a busy schedule. I doubt if he'll see you today."

"You're wrong there, buttercup."

"What?"

Diamond walked over and tried the knob. It was locked.

"I told you. It's private. You'll have to—"

Diamond stepped back, spun, and kicked the door with all his strength. The secretary screamed as the cheap lock tore and the door crashed inward.

Kirk, Piper, Spit, Fifi, and a couple of men Diamond didn't know were sitting around a boat-shaped table.

"It's that maniac. Help!" Piper yelled and covered his head with his hands. "If he ruins my face, it'll cost you millions."

The two men Diamond didn't know—both spectacled

and neither straining the fabric of his double-knit shirt—
jumped up to defend Piper and quickly thought better
of it.

"What's going on?" Kirk demanded.

Diamond looked at Fifi. Her dress was unruffled, her
makeup unsmeared.

"You okay, doll?"

She nodded. "What's this about?"

"Yeah," Kirk added.

"I heard about the parties you have over here, Kirk,"
Diamond said.

"What parties?"

Diamond flipped the picture of Melonie onto the con-
niving record mogul's lap. Kirk looked at it and shrugged.

"I don't know what you're talking about."

Fifi came over to Diamond. She took his arm. "Everything's fine here. You wait outside. I'll be done in a few
minutes."

"Give a holler if you need me," Diamond said reluctantly. "I'll leave the door open."

She looked at the damaged frame. "We don't have
much choice."

He could hear murmurs from the room as he sat in the
outer office, the secretary nervously watching him. Kirk
was agitated, Piper was whining, Spit and the others
mumbled. But Fifi's voice was as soothing as a cold brew
on a hot day.

"Take your blouse off," I told her.

*"But, Red, honey, you just had me get dressed. We
don't have the time to—"*

"Trust me, angel."

*"I do," she said, and again I had a view worth killing
for. I had to make sure it wasn't worth dying for.*

"Stand over here," I said, positioning her so Rocco would get a glimpse of her when he first opened the door.

We didn't have to wait very long.

"Ahhhh," Rocco leered, and I made like a jack-in-the-box with a cannon in either hand.

Another goon drew his gun and I let loose. He was dead before he hit the floor.

Rocco took off down the hall, shouting for the rest of his army of thugs, mugs, pugs, and lugs. I heisted the door opener's piece and barked "Follow me" to Fifi.

I could feel her hands on my back as we ran the gauntlet. It was like one of them shooting galleries where doors pop open and cardboard gunmen stick their faces out. Only this time, the gunmen were real.

As soon as a gun was empty, I'd scoop up another from one of Rocco's boys who had been too slow. The hall seemed longer than Omaha Beach in June of '44. There was as much lead flying.

People say I'm too quick with a rod. I say I was just quick enough. When we reached the door to freedom, my hands were blistered from the heat of the pistols.

Rocco was lying right near the door. I checked his pulse. He had bought the farm, no doubt about it. My long war was over. It was time to hang up my .38 and think about the future.

Fifi and me stepped out into the street. She hadn't gotten a chance to put on a top. I gave her my jacket.

"Oh Red, won't you be cold?"

"I know just the way to warm up," I said as we got into my Packard.

"That's the way the business is," Fifi explained as they leaned against her Mercedes in the Vine-L parking lot. "Business gets taken care of at these things. Throwing a party is an art form."

"This creep Kirk is a pimp."

"These parties are professionally catered, with hired guests, minor celebs, and starlets who make a living showing up and being charming. What better way to encourage men to enjoy themselves than to have available women fawn over them?"

"The real guests don't know?"

"Maybe deep down, but they can pretend they still have animal magnetism, even when their favorite mixed drinks have Geritol in them. Record chain store owners, radio station managers, theater owners, some band managers. Anyone who can do Vine-L good. All the companies do it. Unreported rebates, free trips, payola, drugs, women, boys. It's a sleazy business."

"No wonder Rocco's so interested in it," Diamond said. "But why don't you get out? You got brains, looks, lots going for you. You could leave this racket."

"What? And give up show biz?" she joked.

"It don't sound like much to give up."

"I make better than a hundred grand a year."

He made a low whistle of appreciation. "But are you happy? Wouldn't you like to settle down somewhere, have a few kids, take care of the house while I'm out bringing home the bacon?"

"I hardly know you."

He stepped in and embraced her. "You got to beat that posthypnotic suggestion. I'll get you over it."

She didn't fight, but she didn't respond as he hugged her.

"You're crazy, you know that?"

"Crazy about you. Let's go back to your place."

"Why not yours?"

"There's this kid I'm working with. He's checking things at the library for me. He might come back at any time when he realizes the wild goose chase I sent him on."

"Why'd you do that?"

"He's the brother of that girl in the photo. A good egg, but he knows the streets the way I know Chinese. So I have him checking and cross-referencing the dates, places, and times that rock stars were killed in the past twenty years. I told him I wanted to check them in relation to Edwards and Wynn."

"You are clever," Fifi said, softening in his arms. He pressed his lips to hers. She had gotten her kissing skills back, Red thought.

Chapter Fifteen

"**R**emember that time me and Dan Turner and Shell Scott had to spring you from that orgy Rocco was throwing at the Arabian Nights Club on Melrose?" Diamond asked as he drove west toward Santa Monica.

"I can't say I do."

"You must have a mental block. Of course you was doped. Knucks had slipped you a Mickey Finn. That's how they shanghaied you into that joint. It took me a coupla days to get a lead on Rocco, but then I—"

"Have you ever spoken to anyone professionally about your adventures?"

"Sure. Marlowe, Spade, Archer, Rockford, Gittes. About a dozen of us. We call it the Bloodshot Eyes. Get it?"

She nodded.

"We get together over a few bottles of cheap Scotch and shoot the breeze. You compare notes with your buddies, it helps improve your act. Though I usually spend most of the time talking, with those guys listening. But they appreciate it."

"I presume you're talking about Philip Marlowe and Sam Spade?"

"And Lew Archer, Jim Rockford, J.J. Gittes, Dan Turner. Did I mention Dev Tracy? He comes in from Vegas to join us. Boy, will they be glad to hear that I got you back. We'll go out together and paint the town red."

"What I meant by professionally was a doctor."

"Why? Nothing hurts."

"Maybe someone who would like to listen to your problems, the things that bother you."

"That's why I get together with the Bloodshot Eyes."

"I have a friend, she's very good. She does a lot of rehabilitation of drug addicts, individuals with altered states of reality. You could tell her about these friends of yours. I'm sure she'd waive her fee if I asked."

They stopped for a light. "The only fee I like to see waving is yours," Diamond said, nuzzling her neck.

"I'm serious," she said, pulling away.

"So am I. I don't need my head shrunk. I'm as sane as the President of the United States."

"Who is that?"

"Fifi, I know you never was one for politics, but you should know about FDR. He's been in the White House long enough."

She sighed. "Let's stop by my friend's office. You'll like her."

"I thought we were going to your place?"

"It's on the way."

Red lit a cigarette. Where was Fifi getting these dumb ideas from?

They rode by the chic boutiques and eateries of West Hollywood, to the greenery and flash of Beverly Hills. They were passing the towers of Century City—and Diamond was about to recount an adventure from when it was the Twentieth Century-Fox studio—when he spotted the tail. He stepped on the gas and took the car up to fifty.

"You're going to get a ticket."

"Better a ticket than a bullet."

"That's enough," she said, as he ignored a red light.

144

"This fantasy has got to stop. You're going to get yourself killed. And me along with you. Stop playing around."

"You think this is a game?" Diamond said.

"Yes."

"The game is murder. You remember that case of mine, Scott Marks used that as a title. I don't know how—"

Fifi yelped as they swerved to avoid a bus, hopped on the sidewalk, and came down on the cross street.

Diamond slowed down. "Wait a minute. I just realized something. It's probably that Sean kid again. He did this to me once before."

Fifi was looking out the back window. "I don't see anyone."

"Of course. I lost them."

"That's it. Either let me out here, or promise you'll speak to my friend."

"That kid has gotten better. He's back," Diamond said, eyeballing the rearview mirror.

"Where? What are you talking about?" Fifi said, angrily twisting and peering out the back window.

"The Olds about four cars behind us. It's dark blue. With tinted glass."

"I see it. So what?"

Diamond pounded the gas again, swerved in and out of traffic and made a few sharp turns. The Olds disappeared.

"See," Fifi said.

The Olds reappeared.

"Oh shit," she said.

"He's good, but I'm better," Diamond said. "Fasten your seat belt, toots, it's time for take-off."

Diamond made a few more moves, including a snap-spin U-turn across four lanes of traffic that had enough horns blowing to topple the wall at Jericho. He reached a deserted street and pulled into a cul-de-sac.

The Olds came squealing up as Diamond got out. He walked to the car, ready to chew out the college kid.

There were two men in the Olds. The only college they'd attended had offered courses in license-plate making. They drew their guns.

Diamond ran back to his car as bullets whistled over his head. He started the vehicle and raced off.

"It wasn't who I expected," he said nonchalantly to a very pale Fifi.

"It's true then, about this Rocco," Fifi said as they shrieked down city streets.

"Would I lie to you?" Diamond asked, reaching under his jacket and taking out his .38.

"Can't we go to the police?"

"There's never a copper around when you need one. You got to take care of yourself."

Diamond made another U-turn. He slowed as he passed his pursuers, and squeezed off two shots. One went wild, the other hit the Olds body. The opposition let off four shots, and three hit Diamond's car.

The gunmen made a U-turn and continued their pursuit. But they didn't seem as eager to catch up now that they knew he was armed.

The gas tank needle dropped steadily. "The old Ford is running out of steam. I gotta get you to safety so I can straighten these crumbs out."

"But there's two of them."

"Don't feel too bad for 'em. I'll make it quick."

Fifi kept looking out the window, hoping to not see the Olds, or to see a police car. Neither wish was granted.

The car coughed a few times as they raced down La Cienega. Red-jacketed valets along Restaurant Row stared at the speeding Ford.

"Hey, look at that big place over there," Diamond said, pointing to an eight-level futuristic mud-brown

146

building at the corner of Beverly and La Cienega boulevards.

"That's the Beverly Center."

"What's that?"

"A shopping mall."

Dames always like shopping, Red figured, handing her a twenty. "I'll meet you back here in a half-hour. Buy yourself something nice and flimsy."

"What are you going to do?"

"What I do best."

When the Olds was out of view, he slowed and she hopped from the car. Then he eased back out into traffic, with the fuel gauge a mouse hair away from empty.

The Olds was on his tail. Good. Fifi was safe. The car sputtered. The Olds was gaining as he headed south and crossed back into Beverly Hills.

The air was suddenly filled with sirens, like London when the Luftwaffe was making its nightly visits. Diamond pulled over to the curb in front of La Cienega Park. He didn't have much choice. The Ford was gasping like an asthmatic on a smoggy day.

He leaped from the car, ran a few dozen yards, and hid. The Olds zoomed past. But the gunmen spotted his abandoned auto, braked hard, and slammed into reverse.

From every direction, police cars suddenly roared up. Sheriff's Department, Los Angeles Police Department, Beverly Hills Police Department, California Highway Patrol. Cops, cops, and more cops, a swarm of uniformed men with guns drawn and blood pumping.

Red's pursuers made the mistake of jumping from their car with guns in their hands. Diamond crouched behind a hillock as the bullets began to fly.

In sixty seconds, as many rounds were fired. The pursuers lay dead, two cops were wounded, and the citizens in the area had never been as terrified. Cars slammed into each other as bystanders rubbernecked. The Olds caught

147

fire from a bullet in the gas tank. Fire engines joined the confusion, along with ambulances and a meat wagon from the morgue. TV crews and print reporters raced up. The crowd swelled.

Diamond ditched his gun under a rock and went back to his car. He was parked far enough from the mayhem that no one paid attention. He stuffed a rag into the hole in his tank, walked to the service station on Olympic Boulevard, got gas, went back, and refilled his car.

Special investigation units from the various police departments, as well as the D.A.'s office, had arrived and were trying to figure out what had happened.

A beefy investigator with a clipboard stopped Diamond as he tried to climb into his car.

"Did you see what happened?"

"Nov schmoz ka pop?"

"What?"

"Nov schmoz, nov shmoz. Kretchnik patroosh morkel," Diamond said, pointing furiously at the gas can and his car in the distance.

"Did you see what happened?" the investigator repeated slowly.

Diamond shook his head. "Deedee borkis mitchno."

"Ah, get out of here," the man with the clipboard said, muttering "damn foreigners" as Diamond walked briskly to his car.

Back at the Beverly Center, Fifi waited anxiously.

"Are you all right?" she asked.

"Couldn't be better. The cops finally showed up."

"I know, I called them."

"Huh?"

"I called every department I could think of. I told them an off-duty officer was being chased by dope dealers."

"Oh."

"Don't I at least get a thank you?"

148

"I was hoping to catch them myself. I didn't get to ask the hoods any questions."

"That takes the cake. It really does. I probably saved your stupid life." She handed him back his twenty dollars.

He brushed aside the money and gave her a long kiss. "Thanks," he whispered when they came up for air.

"That's the first time I ever paid anyone for a kiss," she said. "It was worth it."

"I didn't take the money."

"The best things in life are free," she said, and they kissed again.

"We better ditch my jalopy," he said. "It's going to be hot if anyone drops a dime on the chase and the flatfeet put two and two together."

"I'm glad I used to watch George Raft movies. Otherwise I don't think I'd understand you."

"You understand me fine. Let's hole up at your place for a while and I can brush up your parlance."

I closed the door behind us. "Howzabout giving me my jacket back?"

"Indian giver," she said, peeling it off in a way that would make Gypsy Rose Lee and Lili St. Cyr pack away their G-strings.

Her huggable honeydews came into view. The twin peaks were outstanding enough to be a national monument. And they were only two parts of a wonderful whole.

She flipped on the radio and a torch song came on. She moved slowly into my arms, and my fires flared.

"That was incredible," Fifi said, as she and Diamond lay in each other's arms on her brass bed.

"It always is."

"It was like there was nothing else in the world, just you and me."

The P.I. sat up on the edge of the bed and lit a cigarette. "There will be nothing else, cupcake. Once I take care of Rocco."

"Tell me more about him."

Eager to snap her out of the strange state the hypnosis had put her in, Red recounted some of his adventures for an attentive Fifi. He told the stories with such enthusiasm and total recall, she was as hard-pressed to find the edge of reality as he was.

". . . I can still smell the lead in the air as Evans and Rosie charged in. Moe wouldn't give up. He'd gotten the bead on them when I dropped him with a hot poker. Then things got slow for a while, until New York, and now the Edwards and Wynn deaths."

"Who do you think did it?"

"The leads I got are as solid as spring ice. I wouldn't want to go skating on any of 'em."

She ran her fingers down his back. "What angle are you going to follow?"

"I was thinking of staying with you around the clock. Rocco will find out where you are sooner or later and make his move."

"I told you you can't stay with me all the time."

"Why not?"

"I've got a life of my own. You can't barge in and take over."

"All dames want a take-charge joe to handle things."

"Not this one."

"I'll straighten you out, don't worry."

She was silent for a long time. "Maybe you better go."

He embraced her. She was unresponsive, but he was determined. After a few minutes, her resolve had weakened, and they were back under the covers.

"I've got to go to the studio," she said the next morning. "Though I don't feel like leaving."

"Don't. Call in sick."

"I can't. If we don't do the rest of the tracks today, the album might get shelved."

He tried to convince her, but her mind was made up. It's a woman's prerogative to change her mind, Red thought, but don't ever try changing it for her. It was like teaching a mule to tap-dance—it could be done, but it wasn't easy.

He drove her to Vine-L, where she hopped into her car and zoomed off.

"He's not in, he's not in," the strawberry blond secretary said nervously when he appeared at Kirk's office.

Diamond winked at her. "You ought to take a vacation, gorgeous, you're getting too high-strung."

The P.I. drove to his apartment, stopping to pick up a *Herald* from the stand at Las Palmas. He didn't like buying them out of the streetcorner boxes that put the newsies out of business.

He remembered his own days on the windy Chicago streets, hawking the *Trib* during the newspaper wars, when Hearst and rival press moguls hired gangsters to protect their routes. Red and the other kids were caught in the middle.

The headline caught his attention. SHOOT 'EM UP, it said, and underneath, a story by Nat Norris recounted the events near the Beverly Center. The reporter said that the two men in the car were visitors from New York whose names were being withheld pending notification of next of kin. The two injured policemen had been wounded by fellow cops—the New Yorkers hadn't gotten off one shot.

Police were looking into reports that the dead men had been involved in a high-speed chase with another car, as well as the reason for the men to have been illegally carrying firearms.

Diamond drove to a pay phone and called the *Herald*.

"Norris, listen, this is the guy who was involved in the chase over on the West Side."

151

"How do I know that?" the reporter asked, sounding bored.

"You got a description of the other car in the chase?"

"Yeah, but the cops asked me not to use it."

"They tell you it was a late-model Ford sedan, dark brown?"

"Who is this?" Norris's tone had changed. Red felt him trying to climb through the phone.

"Someone who wants to help you."

"What do you want?"

"Anything you can find out about the two dead heavies. Go out and squeeze your sources."

"You mean you don't know who they were?"

"Right. Do you have anything that wasn't in the paper?"

"Promise you won't call the *Times?*"

"You got my word."

Norris recited the information that he either had agreed to withhold or had been cut by the editors. The dead men were Nick Dorceus, forty-six, and Mel Ampus, thirty-one.

"They got priors?"

"Both have arrest records going way back. Assault, arson, B and E, ADW, RSP, a three of homicide arrests between them. The police are convinced they're mob-connected."

"Rocco."

"Who?" the reporter asked. "What was that name?"

"Check your files for a crumbbum named Rocco Rico. This setup has got his fingerprints all over it."

"Would you like to come in and talk? Or maybe meet for a drink somewhere?"

"Don't get too eager. I'll keep in touch."

Diamond hung up before the reporter could ask any more.

Chapter Sixteen

"Boy, my eyes are about ready to fall out of their sockets," Sean said. He was seated at the folding card table in Diamond's kitchen with papers spread out in front of him. "But I finished the research."

"What? There must be hundreds of things to go through."

"Fortunately, I took a speed-reading course at school. And I was lucky I found comprehensive source documents."

"How nice," Diamond said unenthusiastically, retrieving a beer from the fridge.

"You want to take a look?"

Diamond gazed at the pile. "One important thing you got to learn how to do is organize the information into a neat package. You ever watch a federal trial?"

"No."

"You ought to see the way the G-men trot out charts and graphs and visual aids. Organize the papers and then we'll talk."

"But I can give a—"

"It's best, believe me. I'm gonna catch some shut-eye. Why don't you take magic markers and work it up?"

When Red woke from his nap, Sean and his papers

were gone. A note said, "A computer will help speed things up. I'll be back."

Diamond chuckled. That should keep the little beggar busy for a while.

The P.I. remembered his own initiation at the Continental Detective Agency in San Francisco. The Op was making his bones at the same time. They went their separate ways, but still kept in touch, getting together when Diamond was in Frisco, or the Op in L.A., to reminisce about The Old Man and the hard time he'd given them when they were wet behind the ears.

Those days, there weren't speed-reading classes and computers, just old-fashioned legwork. Standing in Chinatown alleys watching smoke curling up from basement opium dens; or perching in a tree on Nob Hill while the rain beat down and the subject of the surveillance feasted inside his mansion; or pretending to be a drunken seaman staggering around North Beach.

Diamond did his push-ups, sit-ups, and jumping-jacks routine, showered, and put on a somber black suit. He drove to Constantine's Mortuary and, using the name Spiros, had a chat about his soon-to-be-departed uncle. Diamond took the funeral director's card and left after receiving the proper amount of heartfelt regret from Mr. Constantine.

He also lifted a chrysanthemum from a flowerpiece in the hallway and tucked it into his lapel.

He drove to the morgue, timing it so that most of the staff was on lunch break. Diamond was a paragon of pomp. He handed his Constantine Funeral Home business card to the receptionist and waved a sheaf of important-looking papers. He was loud enough to dominate, but not so loud as to draw the attention of the skeleton staff of clerical workers at the far side of the room.

The woman behind the counter had plain features, frizzy brown hair, and an unhappy expression. She quickly

154

became flustered as he double-talked and gestured rapidly, explaining that he had come to make arrangements for the funeral of Dorceus and Ampus.

"But Mr. Constantine—"

"I am an artist. When I am done, they will be fit to show in the Parthenon. Their cheeks will flush with a joy Achilles would envy, their clothes will drape them like Athena's gown. I must see them, and their effects. If you will have someone show me the way."

"I'm trying to tell you, the bodies have already been claimed and flown back to New York."

"This is an outrage. Who gave permission? Where did they go?"

"That's confidential information."

"Where is your boss? I will have you cleaning autopsy tables. Get the supervisor."

"He's out to lunch."

"This is vital business. A crime has possibly been committed. I am a personal friend of three of the county supervisors. I must have that information to find out who steals bodies from Constantine."

The woman hesitated.

"Darling, this will be a secret between Nicholas Constantine and you," he said, giving her a gentle chuck under the chin.

"I don't know . . ."

He winked. "You know, you little minx." He lifted a ten from his wallet and the chrysanthemum from his lapel. He wrapped the bill around the flower and handed it to her.

"I can't take this," she said, without much conviction.

"A beautiful lady like yourself should be surrounded by beautiful things. I can understand your not wanting to take any chances. Accept this as a small token of my appreciation for your spending the time to talk to me."

Diamond took a few very slow steps toward the door.

"Wait," she said, and he turned with a quizzical expression on his face.

"I guess it wouldn't hurt to show you the file. Especially if you didn't tell anyone where you got the information."

Diamond blew her a kiss and then zipped his lips shut.

She hurried to a file cabinet and dug out the folder, looking both ways like a spy in a B-movie before setting it down on the counter.

"The autopsy report isn't in there. It's still being typed," she said. "They did this postmortem in a hurry."

"I don't need the report, darling," Diamond said. "However they've passed on, I will take them in."

The bodies were on their way to the Greenview Funeral Home in New York, properly authorized by the authorities and requested by the next of kin, she told him.

"They're getting good treatment."

"I heard Greenview is one of the fanciest in New York," she said.

"They must come from wealthy families. It is a pity I didn't get the honor of laying them to rest."

Diamond thumbed through the forms. On a piece of phone-message paper, he found the number of New York attorney Sharon Rosenthal.

"I wonder who she is?"

"She's been handling the arrangements. That's how things got done so quickly. She's got a lot of clout."

"You've been more than wonderful. Thank you," Diamond said, handing back the file.

He glanced back just before walking through the swinging glass doors. The woman was sniffing the flower and looking off into space.

Diamond went to his office, checked the mail and messages. There were calls from Sharkey and Tartaglia in New York. Neither was in when he called.

Before leaving the office he wrote "Out of Order" on three index cards and pocketed them. He walked to the Wittaker Building. It was of the same vintage as the one housing his office, but better kept. The plants in the lobby were more green than brown.

Mike and Juanita Chavez worked the newsstand in the lobby. Both were blind. Diamond had gotten to know them when he'd caught a well-dressed businessman slipping them a single and saying it was a five.

"I recognize those footsteps," Mike said as Diamond walked to the counter. "You're moving quickly. On an important case?"

"They all are. I need to borrow your wife for a few minutes."

"Any time, big boy," Juanita said in a better than average impression of Mae West. Juanita's hobby was mimicking voices.

"I need a secretary, very efficient, very impressed with herself."

"A bitch," Mike said. "She's been practicing for that part."

She slapped him playfully. "One moment, please, I have to finish doing my nails," Juanita said officiously.

"Perfect."

She came out from behind the counter and took Diamond's arm. "If I'm not back in a day or so, we've run off to Rio," she said.

"If you're not back in fifteen minutes, I'll shoot your dog," Mike said. The German shepherd curled up behind the counter groaned as if he understood. "Only kidding, Marlita. Maybe you and I will run off and leave her."

Diamond and Juanita walked to the bank of pay phones. Diamond put his "Out of Order" signs up.

There were three lawyers' offices in the building that had the same exchange as the pay phones. If the party at the other end checked the number Diamond gave against a

157

listed phone number, they looked like extensions in the same office.

"Are you Ferguson or Levine?" Juanita asked.

"I was Levine last week."

"Ferguson it is. Who am I calling?"

"Sharon Rosenthal, a hotshot New York lawyer."

She dialed and got past the receptionist to Rosenthal's secretary. When Rosenthal got on the line, Juanita handed the phone to Diamond.

"Rosenthal, Fred Ferguson here, how you doing?" Diamond asked, very hail-fellow-well-met.

"Busy, very busy. How can I help you?"

"On the Dorceus-Ampus matter, I understand you're handling things," Diamond said.

"Why does it interest you?"

"One of my clients says he saw the police open fire without any provocation. The victims got out with their hands clearly in the air. I don't know how it is in New York, but there's been some very successful litigation out here, with sizable out-of-court settlements."

"Who's your client?"

"Oh come now, you can't expect me to give that up so quickly."

Diamond tried to get the lawyer to reveal who she was representing; Rosenthal tried to do the same to the P.I. Both got nowhere. They hung up cordially, with Rosenthal promising to call back.

Diamond and Juanita waited by the phones. "No dice," Diamond said after fifteen minutes. He took the "Out of Order" signs down and handed Juanita a twenty.

"You were perfect, as usual."

"Next stop, the Carson show," she said, giving him a peck on the cheek. He led her back to the newsstand, bantered with the couple a bit, and walked to another bank of pay phones a block away.

158

He called the reporter Norris. "Any news?" Diamond asked.

"Yeah, the Pope came out for world peace," Norris cracked, disgustedly. "I checked our files going back sixty years. The only Rocco Rico mentioned was a lounge-act singer in the forties."

"He probably had his file pulled."

"What are you talking about?"

"Rocco's clever that way. He's covered up traces of his identity."

"Is this a gag? Did Markman at the *Times* sic you on me?"

"I got something for you and it's no gag. The stiffs were given speedo treatment out of the coroner's office," Diamond said. He could hear Norris's fingers dancing across the typewriter. "You got any buddies at the New York papers?"

"A few."

"Have 'em check the clips for a Sharon Rosenthal. An attorney."

"How's she figure in?"

"You find out her clients, I'll let you know the skinny."

"How do I know you're not sending me on a wild goose chase?"

"Don't I have an honest voice?"

"No."

"Well, maybe they'll think so at the *Times*."

"Okay, okay. You twisted my arm."

Back in his office in the Carlin Building, Diamond tried Sharkey and Tartaglia again. The rock entrepreneur still wasn't in, but the lawyer was. He told him the divorce was proceeding smoothly and itemized the property Milly was claiming.

159

"I never heard of any of that junk," Diamond said after hearing the list. "Give it all to her. I don't have time to get involved with screwball dames. Besides, I found Fifi."

"How did that come about?"

"She was hiding under the name Penelope Chance. But we knew each other as soon as we met."

Tartaglia questioned Diamond about Fifi—where and how they met, did she work, and if so, where, and where she lived.

"Why the cross-examination?" he asked.

"Nichols might try to use it on Milly's behalf. Alienation of affections."

"I've always been faithful to Fifi. I may look at other tomatoes, but I don't squeeze them."

"That's good. You don't want tomato sauce staining your clothing."

"By the way, you ever heard of a lawyer named Sharon Rosenthal?"

"Sure. She's a big-gun criminal type. Why?"

"You know any of her clients?"

"Not personally. Most are the sort you wouldn't want to meet in a dark alley. Or a bright park. Or anywhere without police protection."

"Any names come to mind?"

"Well, the most obvious one is Sidney Becker."

"What?"

"She's been Becker's criminal lawyer for years."

"Things are starting to fall into place."

"What are you talking about?"

"Only murder, chum."

The P.I. heard the footsteps out in the hall. It was a man's tread, someone who moved fast on his feet. Red slid open the desk drawer where he kept the spare .38 and waited. Through the opaque glass, he saw the figure stop

160

in front and read the name on the door—Red Diamond: Private Eye.

The P.I.'s hand drifted to the butt of the revolver as the door opened.

"Hi, Dad," Sean said cheerily.

Diamond closed the drawer. "Listen, kid, you got lots of energy and you're doing the right thing by your sister. You got spunk. But can't you find someone else to call Dad?"

"Sorry. Anyway, it's all done. A salesman at the computer store let me work on one of their machines for free, after I showed him how to reprogram the PC to translate Basic to Cobol without CP/M problems and re——"

"You organized everything?" Diamond asked incredulously.

"It was simple," Sean said, taking out neatly lined graphs and charts. He sat in the client's chair opposite Diamond's desk and began talking enthusiastically:

"I used standard actuarial tables to calculate the odds of these deaths being coincidental. The odds of it happening purely by chance worked out to 347,292 to one. The oldest person I found was Elvis Presley, who died of a heart attack at forty-two in Tennessee. The youngest was Sid Vicious, who died at twenty-one in New York. Heroin overdose. The average age was twenty-seven, the median age was——"

"Enough, enough, I see you did your homework. Did you find any patterns?"

"Geographically the deaths are scattered. London, Paris, New York, California, Wisconsin, Mississippi. I cross-collated the climate and also turned up nothing. Ninety-eight percent of the victims were male, seventy-two percent were white. The causes of death varied, with drug overdoses and plane crashes claiming the lion's share, though there were a few heart attacks, motorcycle accidents, drownings, electrocutions, shootings, suicide, and one, Mama Cass, choking to death on a piece of food. In the Jim Morrison case, there's a question of whether it was pneumonia or—"

"Any conclusions?" Diamond asked, lighting a cigarette.

"You don't want to hear about Morrison? How about Bobby Fuller, who supposedly killed himself by drinking gasoline, though some people say—"

"I'll look over the specifics later. Right now, I need the big picture. Give me the first you found."

"Most materials use the 1959 plane crash of Buddy Holly as the first death. Two other rock notables, Richie Valens and the Big Bopper, died in Iowa in that crash."

"You said 'most materials'? Were there any others?"

"There was some reference to a Dickie Rogers. In late 1958 he was shot to death in his home after his record 'She's My Cuddly Baby' went platinum. It was dismissed as a burglary gone sour."

"What do you know about it?"

"The house was completely torn up so that no exact inventory could be taken. Rogers was a poor kid who had unlimited money for the first time in his life, and no one knew exactly what he had bought. He had a brand-new car parked in the living room of his house. Although a substantial amount of goods were reported missing, there were valuables lying around that the burglar should've taken."

"Was he married?"

"No. He had a childhood sweetheart he had been engaged to, but apparently the relationship was on the rocks. Lots of women wanted to be his cuddly-baby."

"Sounds like a good lead. Why don't you run it down?"

"But the trail is more than twenty-five years old! I wasn't even born when it happened."

"You got to begin in the beginning."

"How can I find any of these people?"

162

"Where'd you get the information on him?"

"Various places. A book on fifties rock, a few magazine articles."

"Call the publishers and get a way to contact the writers. Ask them. You can't be expected to be an expert in everything, but you oughta be able to find an expert in anything."

That should keep the kid busy, Red thought. Nothing better than putting him in touch with a pack of long-winded authors.

The P.I. retrieved his desk bottle, took a slug, and began making calls.

"Vine-L Records, Mr. Kirk's office," the cold-blooded secretary answered.

"Is Kirk in?" the P.I. asked.

She recognized his voice and her own went up an octave. "No. He's not. I don't know when he will be."

"Thanks."

He hung up and called Sharkey.

"What's been going on?" Sharkey asked. "I been trying to get ahold of you."

"I been trying to reach you too. Wynn went to join Edwards in rock-and-roll heaven."

"I heard. I want you to stick with Piper twenty-four hours a day."

"That's liable to get cozy at bedtime," Diamond cracked. "You don't sound real busted up over Wynn's death."

"You want phony emotion? Edwards's death was a loss to humanity. Wynn getting killed was bad for business. If anything happens to Peter before we finish the album, I'm in trouble."

"Your concern for him is touching. You ought to get another P.I. to do it. I can recommend some good ones. I haven't seen Marlowe doing much recently."

"But you're familiar with the problem."

"Piper and I didn't exactly hit it off."

"I know. He called and said something about a maniac assaulting him. I assumed he was exaggerating, until I heard from Kirk."

"You know about the parties at Vine-L?"

"No."

"It'll be in my report. Anyway, I figure I'm better on the outside. If someone is out to whack him, I'm better off going after them than waiting around like a sitting duck."

"Mr. Diamond, please, stay with Peter the next day or so. After we finish the album, he'll be taking off for his retreat in Baja. I'll give you a five-thousand-dollar bonus."

"When you appeal to my sentimental instincts like that, how can I say no?"

Chapter Seventeen

The P.I. drove to Vine-L, where the strawberry blonde tried to convince him Kirk wasn't around. Diamond ignored her and walked in on Kirk and another man.

"Mr. Diamond, I've been looking forward to seeing you," Kirk said, as friendly as a used-car salesman.

Diamond lit a cigarette. "Can the sweet talk, mushmouth. Let's get down to business."

"That will be all, Barry," Kirk said to the other man, who looked at the angry Diamond and hurried from the room. Barry closed the repaired door behind himself as he left.

"What can I do for you?" Kirk asked.

"I left a picture of a girl and a guy with you."

"It wasn't much of a shot of the man. From his salami down."

Diamond walked over to Kirk's desk and loomed over him. "Where can I find her?"

"How should I know?"

"You booked her here for a party."

"Another girl brought her."

"Who?"

"I don't remember."

Diamond grabbed Kirk by his shirt and jerked him

across the desk, knocking over a cup of coffee and messing up his papers.

"The woman's name is Busty Betsy. Does that get you remembering or do I have to knock some sense into your head?"

"Yeah, that's her, right. How much do you know?"

"More than enough to put you in jail for a few years. I know about the pimping, the kickbacks, the drugs, the whole shebang. I got sworn affidavits documenting everything."

"We can make a deal. Have you ever thought about a singing career?"

"Where I come from, only stoolies sing. Now, what about the girl in the photo? Do you have a number for her?"

"I don't. But I put her in touch with an agency. Just to be nice. She needed guidance. She was balling everybody for nothing."

Diamond shook Kirk like he was a drink that needed mixing.

"That's my daugh——daugh——daugh——" he began. "I'm looking for her. Where do I find her?"

"I told you, I don't know."

"Who did you refer her to?" Diamond growled between clenched teeth.

"The Action Agency. They're an escort service over on Cahuenga near Sunset. Ralph Goodfellow owns it."

Diamond threw Kirk back into his chair.

Kirk reached into a desk drawer. Diamond slammed it shut on his hand. Kirk screamed. Diamond opened the drawer and took out a 9mm automatic.

"A tough guy, huh?" Diamond asked.

"I keep that for protection," Kirk said shrilly. "Give it back."

"Who do you need protection from?"

"None of your business."

"I can make it my business."

"I'll have you fired," Kirk said, threateningly lifting up the phone.

"If you can get Sharkey to fire me, do it. I don't much give a damn about you or Piper."

Kirk hung up the phone. "I'm not so bad. We can get along. You want to bury the hatchet?"

"I don't like pimps, whether they work off street corners or corporate offices. You stink and your whole racket stinks."

"Everybody does it. Were you telling the truth about having those sworn affidavits?"

"Think about it tonight when you're trying to sleep."

Diamond drove over to the Action Agency. It was located on the third floor of a walk-up building with a shiny facade and a rundown interior. The street-level store sold Hollywood memorabilia, flotsam and jetsam from movies that were worth whatever the storeowner said they were worth.

Walking up the stairs, Diamond passed suites belonging to a dentist, a financial consultant, and a sewer cleaner who billed himself as "The Drain Surgeon— Plumbing Specialist to the Stars."

The top floor only had room for one office, and that one had belonged to the Action Agency. The door was locked. He shook it in its frame, but nothing happened.

Diamond found a suitable lockpick conveniently hanging from the wall and labeled FIRE AXE.

The red axe felt good in his hand and reminded him of Kirk's offer to bury the hatchet. He hefted it once or twice and put the edge in between the door and its frame, right near the lock.

It crunched open like there was a doorman waiting for a tip.

The office was empty. Either Goodfellow had found a

way to keep his overhead lower than even Diamond could, or he had moved out.

The room nearest the door would be where a secretary sat, kept company by a couple of file cabinets, Red figured, eyeing the marks on the linoleum like an Indian scout. Behind a door marked PRIVATE was a larger room. The only item left was a green plastic garbage bag in the middle of the floor.

A thin woman's arm was sticking out of the bag. Diamond drew his gun. He approached cautiously and gently opened the bag.

The arm belonged to an inflatable doll, the kind lonely men kept in their closets. It looked like someone had taken a bite out of the plastic around her throat. Diamond threw the doll down and let out the breath he had been holding.

He dumped the bag and used the tip of his toe to separate the debris.

A postmarked envelope was two days old, so Goodfellow had cleared out recently. From other garbage he learned Goodfellow, or his secretary, smoked Marlboros, drank Gallo wine, liked chop suey, and gulped gallons of java from styrofoam cups. A piece of memo paper with printing—"From the Desk of Ralph Goodfellow"—had a few phone numbers and women's names written on it. It was the only trash he pocketed.

There were publicity stills Goodfellow had gotten from hopefuls. They depicted a homely lot of females, posed glamorously, and often looking painfully awkward. There were phone numbers and addresses scrawled on the backs. Many of the women lived in midwestern towns with names like Freedom, Shady Creek, and Pleasantville. Local numbers were for less prosaically named areas, some of the meaner streets of Los Angeles.

From dirt and pressure marks on the wall and floor, he was able to figure out where Goodfellow had a couch— no doubt the proverbial casting couch—desk, and chairs.

One wall had been covered with pictures. Probably shots of Goodfellow sidling up to minor celebrities, with the celeb's signature forged in a warm dedication.

Diamond canvassed the other businesses in the building. The dentist and financial consultant raved about a never-ending stream of attractive women going to Goodfellow's office. According to the dentist, Goodfellow never represented any women he hadn't tried out personally, wink wink, nudge nudge.

The plumber—who owned the building—had a thin build, but hands that looked like he wouldn't need a monkey wrench to unscrew a rusted pipe. He clenched and unclenched his powerful paws as he talked about Goodfellow.

"I felt bad renting to him. I knew what his business was. Some of the girls was no older than my daughters."

On the plumber's cluttered desk were photos of his wife and daughters. They wore cowboy hats and were posed in front of a corral.

"I seen the girls going up there and coming down an hour or so later. They were," he hesitated, "different. I used to work on a ranch before I came here. Horses would look that same way, right after we'd break 'em."

"Got any idea where I could find him?"

"I wish I did. He skipped out owing three months' rent."

"The studio is closed," the voice at the other end of the intercom said.

"Don't give me that. I'm here to see Fifi."

"There's no one here by that name. Go away."

"Open up or I'll kick it in."

The door opened, but it wasn't the haggard man who had been his guide previously. The doorman was a three-hundred-pound Samoan with a baseball bat in his hand and a wicked gleam in his eye.

Could Rocco have taken over the studio, Red wondered as he drew his .38.

"Out of the way or I'll pitch you a lead fastball," Diamond said, but the batter didn't move.

"What's going on?" the haggard man asked, drifting up from the back.

"Tell Babe Ruth to step aside. I'm here to see Fifi and I'll kill anyone that tries to stop me."

"There's nobody here named Fifi," the haggard man said.

"I know she is. She's with that smart aleck, Piper."

"You mean Penelope?"

"Okay, Penelope."

The haggard man began laughing suddenly, and the Samoan joined in. Diamond didn't understand what was so funny. He shoved past them. He could smell the pungent odor of marijuana clinging to their clothes. Hopheads!

Diamond kept his gun out as he walked down the hall. He ripped the door to Studio A open, startling three heavyset gospel singers and their engineer.

He passed another door and threw it open. Two teenage girls, both in tube tops and hot pants, were sitting on a sofa sharing a reefer. Their eyes got as big as the plastic hoop earrings they wore when they saw the gun. Each tried to pass the joint to the other.

Diamond took the muggle and crushed it under his foot. "The next thing you know, you'll be shooting heroin," he warned. As he left, the girls exploded with laughter.

Piper, Cliff, and Fifi were coming out of Studio B. Piper saw the gun first, and hid behind Cliff. Fifi stepped forward.

"You okay?" Diamond asked Fifi.

"Fine. Unless you shoot me."

"Not with this thing," he said, holstering the weapon. "They gave me a hard time. I thought you might be in trouble."

170

"He's nuts!" Piper yelled, still hiding behind Cliff. The engineer looked at Diamond and Fifi, shrugged, and walked to the lounge, which was equipped with a vending machine, video game, coffeemaker, and microwave.

"Peter, you're not making things any easier," Fifi chided. "Why don't you go relax?"

Edging nervously around Diamond, Piper made a beeline to the office where the two girls waited. He hung a DO NOT DISTURB sign on the door as he shut it behind himself.

"Is he going to—"

"Red, anything is legal in a recording studio, as long as the album gets done."

"Those girls are underage dope addicts."

"Trust me. They're both eighteen. The only thing they do is a little marijuana."

"Where do they come from?"

"Haven't you ever heard of groupies?"

"Are they like bobby-soxers?"

"Sort of. But they do more than just scream. There was one group, called the Plaster Casters, who, uh . . . never mind. What's going on?"

"I'm supposed to bodyguard Piper. Talk about having mixed emotions about a job."

"If you don't want to, Kirk sent over someone."

"The hulk with the baseball bat? What's his pedigree?"

"He's a thumper. Done a lot of concert security. You know, the guard who stands in front of the stage, throwing overexcited fans back into the audience?"

"He hasn't learned that God made men, but Colonel Colt made them equal. I nearly had to teach him. Besides, he's a drug fiend. This whole place is filled with 'em. You better watch out they don't put it in the water."

"I'll be okay. I'm a big girl now."

"In all the right places."

"What about Peter?" she said as he tried to hug her.

"I'll be his bodyguard. It'll be an education. For him."

"Where are you going?" she asked as he moved away.

"To go fetch the body to guard."

Diamond walked to the room with the DO NOT DIS-TURB sign and knocked.

"Go away," Piper's voice yelled from inside.

"Open up."

"Never."

Diamond stepped back and opened the door with a solid kick. Piper was on the sofa between the teenagers. He had stripped down to a pair of bright blue bikini briefs and his lizard-skin cowboy boots. The girls wore only their earrings. They all held glasses filled with an amber fluid.

"Bitchin'," one of them said.

"To the max," the other agreed.

Piper fell to the floor on his knees. "Please, leave me alone," he said, accidentally knocking the bottle of Amaretto over.

"What's this?" Diamond asked, ignoring the rock star and picking up the bottle. "Any of you drink this?"

"We were going to. Until you came in," Piper said. "If we give you some, would you go away?"

"Where'd it come from?"

"The chicks brought it for me," Piper said.

"Didn't anyone ever tell you not to take candy from strangers?" Diamond said. He turned to the girls. "Which liquor store sold you minors the booze?"

"Well, like we didn't actually go and *buy* it," one groupie said.

"This old lady gave it to us," the other added.

"Totally aged."

"What did she say?" Diamond asked.

"She saw us hanging out outside and asked us if we were here for Peter."

"We told her, for sure," the other said. "She said she

was a fan of his from way back, and could we, you know, give him this drink for her."

Diamond sniffed the Amaretto, walked over to a potted plant, and poured the liquor into it.

"Hey!" Piper complained. "That was mine."

"I ought to let you drink it. Smell this," he said, giving Piper the bottle.

The rock star sniffed. "Smells like almonds."

"Don't it smell bitter for a sweet liqueur?"

"You saying it's a cheap brand?"

"I'm saying it's poison. Cyanide."

Piper gulped loud enough to register on the Richter scale and quickly handed the bottle back to Diamond, as if touching the glass could be dangerous. The girls' mouths dropped, forming perfect lipsticked ovals.

"How . . . how did you know?"

"I had a case like this before. In Chicago. I worked with Nate Heller. A former speak called 'The Blind Pig.' Frank Nitti had met his maker, and an honest joe tried to run this Pig joint. A salesman came around, with samples of Amaretto. Free. I was suspicious. Nothing's free unless you pay for it. I followed him. He was one of Rocco's boys. It's a long story."

"You saved my life," Piper kept repeating.

"Wow . . . totally awesome . . . far out . . . like fan-fucking-tastic," the teens said.

"Now, tell me about this old woman," Diamond ordered the girls.

"She was ancient."

"Definitely," the other echoed. "Like, fifty years old."

"Can you gimme a better description?"

The girls had paid great attention to what she was wearing—a yellow chiffon outfit that was completely out of fashion. She had brown hair and brown eyes and a good complexion, they noted. They couldn't describe the car she was driving, only that it looked "classy."

The shock of nearly being poisoned was wearing off, and the drugs in their systems took over. They began to get giggly again.

"Get dressed and go home," Diamond said.

"Shouldn't we call the police?" Piper asked.

"I wanna keep this quiet. But if you want it known that someone tried to poison you while you romped with this jailbait, it's your business."

"Get dressed," Piper told them. "You better go."

Piper put on his clothes and wandered from the room.

"One question," Diamond asked the girls. "How did you know he would be here?"

The girls exchanged looks.

"We're not supposed to say."

"Don't you figure someone who saves your life is entitled?"

They exchanged looks again.

"Dying means no more new clothes, no more boys, no more Mary Jane," the P.I. said.

"Ralph sent us."

"Ralph who?"

"Ralph Goodfellow."

PART THREE

Chapter Eighteen

The girls didn't have any leads on Goodfellow. They had been "interviewed" by him several months earlier at his Cahuenga Boulevard office. Since then he had sent them to parties where they had met a truckload of celebrities and rock stars whose names meant nothing to Diamond.

All roads were pointing to Goodfellow. But who was the "ancient" dame with the deadly gift? Why did Kirk have a gun? Who murdered Wyatt Edwards, if it was a homicide? Who was the hit-and-run driver who squooshed Charlie Wynn? What happened to Amelia Earhart and Judge Crater? Red couldn't spend the time babysitting Piper while the questions danced around his head like Ginger Rogers and Fred Astaire.

Fifi ran in and threw her arms around him. "Peter told me what you did. That was a fantastic bit of detective work."

"Piece a cake."

"Peter is on the phone to Sharkey. He wants you to move into his mansion, stay with him around the clock."

"So he loves me. Great."

"Stick with him, Red. We only need another few days in the studio."

177

"I got to tie up some loose ends."

"For me?" she asked, coming into his arms. Her hair had a sweet smell, like freshly mowed grass.

The groupies were watching like it was a soap opera.

"Beat it," Diamond said, and they hurried out.

He returned to nuzzling Fifi.

"We'll get him on his way to his place in Baja, and then I'll be able to thank you for all you've done," she said.

"You don't need to thank me."

"But I want to," she said, giving him a kiss that sent his pulse up higher than a V-2. "I'll thank you for days."

Diamond saw that Piper was safely locked into the studio. The P.I. sat for a while in the control booth with Fifi and Cliff, but then Piper's wailing got on his nerves, and he went for a cup of coffee.

He met Spit in the snack room.

"Hear anything about Melonie?" Diamond asked.

"Nope."

"What are you here for?" Diamond asked.

"Just going over the studio. My group's going to cut a demo here."

"For Vine-L?"

"No. Kirk's too much of a crook. When we met there yesterday I was on my way to kiss him off."

"Maybe I was a little rough with you."

"If that's an apology, I accept."

"So you're looking for a record company?"

"I'm using my own money for this album. If it takes off, then I can get one of the majors to distribute it just as well as Kirk can."

"I had heard Kirk was a crook from way back. You musta known that. You been around."

"Off the record?" Spit asked, grinning as he tapped a gold record on the wall.

"Off the wall, off the record."

"I didn't mind it when he cheated to help his artists. Now he's screwing them, too. He bootlegs his own records."

"Huh?"

"Say a hundred thousand albums are supposed to be pressed. He has an extra ten thousand done and puts them into black-market distribution channels."

"What about the raw materials? The vinyl, the labels?"

"Listed in inventory as damaged."

"How'd you find this out?"

"I was at the pressing plant. A worker on the loading dock turned out to be a fan of my old group. He thought it was lousy to rip off the artists' royalties like that."

"Is your name really Spit?"

"I was born Rodney Hemphill."

"I'll call you Spit," the P.I. said, giving a two-fingered salute as he took his coffee back to the sound stage.

Piper kept blowing the lyrics, or his voice would crack, or he would slip off-key. After an hour of attempts, Fifi pulled the plug on the session.

What happened between me and my honeybunch ain't nobody's business but ours, and anyway, I don't want to make every Tom, Dick, and Harry jealous.

After three days of making whoopee, we ran out of food, and I decided to go out and grab us some grub.

I left her under the covers, with her promise to do something special to me when I got back.

You can imagine how fast I went through the store. A few cans of this, a few bottles of that, lots of good red meat to give me strength, a few cartons of smokes. I paid the bill and hurried back faster than Sandy on his way to save Little Orphan Annie.

Fifi was gone and my place looked like a cyclone hit it.

Diamond had Piper call the staff together. Besides Babette, the maid Diamond had already seen, two other voluptuous women also served Piper. There was Nita, the cook, and Ginger, the handywoman-groundskeeper.

Nita was a statuesque black woman who looked as delicious as a piece of freshly baked chocolate blackout cake. Her eyes had a vaguely Oriental cast, her mouth shaped in a half-smile, giving her an air of perpetual mystery. With a little makeup, she could have easily gone on the cover of a high-fashion magazine.

Ginger was in her mid-fifties, but she had a vitality and energy that made her ageless. Her long hair had as many gray strands as black. Her hazel eyes burned with promise of wild passion, like Acquanetta, the Jungle Woman.

"If you want her, she's yours," Piper whispered to Diamond. "Not only is she great in bed, but she can fix a stereo, a BMW, or a garbage disposal. She's got great hands." He gave Diamond a smug grin.

"You're a disgusting creep, you know that?" Diamond said and walked away.

Piper followed him. "What did I do? What did I do?"

"You don't give away dames like a wardheeler handing out turkeys."

"But I pay her well. She's happy."

"How long has she been with you?"

"Close to a year," Piper said. "She worked for Howie Janson before that."

"Who's he?"

"Who's he? Howie Janson, as in Howie and the Heartbreakers. He had six platinum records and twice that many gold."

"Why'd she leave him?"

"He died. Right in the middle of a concert. It started raining. There was a short circuit. He wrapped his hand around the mike and got a thousand volts. Anyway, Penelope arranged for Ginger to come here. It was the best thing she'd done for me."

"What about Nita?"

"She's been with me seven, eight years. Cooks the most delicious kielbasa of anyone outside of my mother."

Piper covered his mouth. "You won't tell anyone."

"Tell what?"

"I might as well confess."

"I ain't a priest."

"My real name isn't Piper. It's Pulaski."

"The man who screws maids, high-schoolers, and anything that doesn't have a beard is confessing his deep dark secret."

"Nobody knows I'm Polish," Piper said. "I grew up in Chicago. My old man worked in a distillery."

He gushed out a story of a boring childhood, a normal adolescence, and an uninspired young manhood. Although he acted as if he was revealing an exciting saga, Piper's autobiography would've cured the most virulent insomniac.

"I was a virgin until I was nineteen, do you believe that?" Piper said, as introduction into stories of first lusts and loves.

"Yeah, but I also believe in the Easter bunny."

Piper continued with his recital, and Diamond half listened, hoping there would be something relevant. There wasn't.

"That was fascinating," Diamond said, taking Piper's elbow and leading him upstairs. "But I got work to do. I want you to stay in your room and not let anyone in."

"What happens if any of my groupies show up?"

"They'll have to get by by tucking your glossy under their pillow."

"Babette? Nita?"

"No."

"Ginger?"

"No. Either me or Penelope will bring you food."

181

"But she won't go to bed with me. I tried, believe you me."

"You're lucky."

"What do you mean?"

"If you had done it, I might bring you a bottle of Amaretto."

Piper's room was the size of the Paramount Theater. His canopied bed was as big as the stage, and probably had been host to as many performances.

The walls were decorated with enormous murals showing Piper's favorite artist. Himself, singing, dancing, hamming it up for the camera. The mammoth furnishings looked like they'd been lifted from a castle. Red wondered if the Queen of England was missing her bureau.

"What do you think?" Piper asked proudly.

"You live here alone or does the 82nd Airborne bunk down when they're not in the field?"

Piper went over to a bank of stereo gear that rivaled the equipment Diamond had seen at the recording studio. "Listen to this," Piper said, putting on one of his old records. "Isn't that great?" he asked, as "Righteous Revolution" blasted from four-foot-high JBL acoustic-suspension speakers.

Piper was wailing something about throwing away your possessions and running bare-ass down the streets.

Piper wasn't waiting for Diamond's answer. He was sitting in front of the speakers, listening to his own voice like the RCA dog. Diamond walked over and shut the stereo.

"Hey!"

"You can listen to it later. First I got to give you a few tips on staying alive."

That got Piper's attention.

"Don't go near the windows. Try and keep it as dark as you can in here. You stand framed in the window with a strong light behind you, it's like wearing a 'shoot me' sign.

When you answer the door, stand off to one side, so no one can pump lead through the wood and into you. Finally, don't open the door for nobody but me or Fifi."

"Fifi? Is that some hot number you're going to send up for me?"

Diamond slapped him again.

"Why'd you do that?" Piper asked, holding his reddening cheek.

"You don't talk that way about my Fifi."

"Your Fifi? Oh, you mean Penelope, right? But what about a little female companionship for me?"

"You got a bathroom here?"

Piper pointed.

"Take lots of cold showers."

Diamond made a complete circuit of the house and grounds. It took him more than an hour and he moved briskly. He came upon Ginger cleaning the pool. She offered to walk with him and answer his questions.

Piper's estate had high, solid stone fences, topped by three strands of barbed wire. The pressure-sensitive top wire was tied to a deluxe alarm system that included sensors on all windows and doors. There was a panic button in every room, and floodlights on the grounds that could turn back the night.

Ginger told him about the system as she led him to the stables, which also served as the kennel. Piper had four Rottweilers, obedience- and attack-trained, who patrolled the grounds at night. Only she and Piper could control them.

When they reached the hedge gardens, Ginger suddenly seized Diamond and pressed her lips to his. They were hot, like she was burning with a fever. She ground her lithe body against him.

"Take me, take me here," she said, leading him to a

wooden bench. Diamond sat upright as she lay back and unbuttoned her top.

"Sweetheart, you could melt the paint off a battleship," Diamond said. "But there's two things keeping me from a romp in the hay."

"What?" she asked breathlessly.

"One, I can't get involved with no one here until this Piper pickle gets straightened out."

"What's the other?"

"I got someone."

"But she doesn't care. I know her."

She sat up and ran her hands over his chest. "Relax. I'll take care of everything."

He stood up. "Thanks for the tour."

"Fag bastard," she snarled.

"You know, you're beautiful when you're mad."

The hot water felt good as it battered Diamond's sore muscles. He had worked up a hard sweat with his exercise routine, bolstered by jogging five times around the estate.

He was singing "Ac-cent-tchu-ate The Positive" when Fifi came in. They didn't say anything as she climbed into the shower with him. They didn't need to. They were wet flesh slipping and sliding against each other.

"I remember when I always had to be the one to start things," Diamond said, as he scrubbed her back afterwards. "I like the change."

"You talk about someone who isn't me."

"Don't worry, honeybunch, it's the hypnotism."

"I was never hypnotized."

"That's what they made you believe."

He said it with such intensity and conviction that Penelope nearly found herself doubting her own recollection.

He pressed against her and licked a few water droplets from her neck.

184

"Red, I came here to tell you you better go. It's dangerous for you around here." She pushed his hands away.

"It's dangerous for me everywhere."

"I'm serious."

"So am I," he said, resuming his fondling.

"Please, for my sake, go," she said, stepping out of the shower. "You don't realize what you've gotten into."

"Have you heard from Rocco?"

"Will you stop it with this Rocco nonsense. This isn't a game. You're going to get killed."

He shut the shower and got out. Fifi, in her naked splendor, stood dripping on the tile floor. He put his arms around her gently and they dripped together.

"Don't worry, angel. Red Diamond can take care of himself."

"I was attracted to you because you were different from anyone I had ever met. Sweet and silly and funny and brave. Smart and dumb, cruel and kind."

"Sounds like you're about to write a song."

"I can't bear to see you get killed."

"Level with me, doll, what's eating you?"

Her lush lips parted and quivered. No words came out. She leaned against him and cried. He stroked her sodden hair, then used a bath towel to daub the water from her face and body.

"You'll feel better. A good cry cleans the system," he said.

"If you love me at all, you'll get out of here," she said, as they both dressed.

"Red Diamond doesn't get scared and give up. If I let Rocco off the hook, he'll keep making our lives miserable. Not that being with you could ever be miserable. What I'm saying is I'm on to something, and I got to play out my hand."

She turned and stormed out.

Diamond checked in on Piper, who was raptly listen-

185

ing to an album of his group's greatest hits. On a silver tray in front of him was filet mignon, a pile of diced fancy vegetables, and a decanter of wine.

"Who gave you the food?"

"Nita."

"Did I tell you it was safe to eat?"

"Oh, come on. She's been with me for years."

"Maybe she never had someone offer her a grand to sneak strychnine in your vino?"

Piper spat out a mouthful of wine. "She wouldn't, would she?"

"It's your life. You don't want to listen to me, you make me look like a schmuck, but you turn up under a field of posies."

He shoved the tray aside.

"We have the cook prepare dinners, then we see who eats what by drawing straws."

"I can't believe this."

"Believe it."

Diamond had reached the door when Piper cleared his throat. "Uh, Red."

"Yeah."

"Thanks."

"All in the line of duty."

Fifi was waiting at the foot of the curving staircase, holding a phone up for Diamond. It was Sharkey.

"You're fired," he said.

"What?"

"I hate to break it to you rough, but I don't believe in beating around the bush."

"You got any particular reason, or you decided Piper is worth more to you dead? Maybe you can re-release the group's old albums?"

"That's a low blow."

"From what I've seen out here, you people go lower than a German U-boat."

186

"I'll write you out a check."

"That's fine."

"I don't owe you an explanation, but I'll give you one anyway. Kirk is shook up. So is Penelope, Peter, everyone connected with this venture. I need a delicate touch out there. It's more than a one-man operation."

"So you calling in a bunch of ballerinas?"

"I'm sorry you're taking this so badly."

"Me? Take it badly? You want it quiet out here? Wait until your star gets bumped off, then you'll see what quiet is. I got news for you about Kirk. He's—"

Diamond heard the doorbell ring.

"Wait!" he shouted, but Babette had already opened it. Three burly beach-boy types in dark suits stood in the doorway. They had a commanding physical presence and bulges under their jackets.

Diamond dropped the phone and drew his gun.

The beach boys moved quick. Diamond was looking down the wrong end of two Uzis and an Ingram machine pistol.

Babette fainted.

From the earpiece of the phone, Sharkey's voice sounded tinny as he kept repeating, "What's going on, what's going on?"

"Drop the gun," a beach boy ordered.

"Where's Rocco?" Diamond said. "Or don't he have the nerve to face me?"

"Rocco?" the beach boys asked in unison.

"What's going on?" Sharkey kept repeating through the phone.

"Don't play cute with me," Diamond said, keeping his .38 aimed at the middle beach boy. "You're gonna have to kill me before you get to my client, and I'm taking at least one of you with me."

Fifi stepped into the middle of the battlefield. "Are you the gentlemen that—"

187

"Fifi, get out of the way!" Diamond shouted. His finger was white on the trigger. She was right in the line of fire.

One of the beach boys shoved her to the side. "You ought to be more careful, miss."

"Who are you?" Fifi demanded.

"I'm Biff. My partners are Buzzy and Dean. We're part of Pacific Security. Mr. Sharkey contacted us."

"Oh yeah?" Diamond said challengingly. Still keeping an eye and gun barrel on them, Diamond lifted the phone.

"Sharkey, I got three bozos here with enough hardware to do a replay of the St. Valentine's Day Massacre. They say you ordered them."

"Pacific Security must've sent them over early."

After a few more tense moments, identification was shown and guns were lowered. Babette was revived. Diamond and the beach boys continued to glare at each other.

Piper came bounding down the stairs. "That was incredible," he said to Diamond. "You faced up to all that firepower. You would've died to save me."

"It ain't you, it's the principle. And what are you doing out of your room?"

"I heard the commotion. I'm going to write a song about this. A tribute."

Piper bounded up the stairs.

"Wow, what an honor," one of the beach boys said.

Diamond rolled his eyes and took Fifi's hand. "C'mon, let's go."

"I can't. I have to stay."

Diamond looked around. The occupants of the house, except for Piper, had gathered in the entrance foyer.

"No one can make you stay."

"I want to."

"No you don't. Come with me."

"If you don't want to go, we'll escort him from the premises," the biggest beach boy said.

188

"How'd you like a surfboard up your keister?" Diamond snarled.

Diamond couldn't convince her. The beach boys began to get restless. The servants watched silently. Ginger's eyes glistened. The atmosphere was tenser than a Hatfield-McCoy family picnic.

"Come into the kitchen with me, Red," Fifi said. "We can talk."

He followed his lady love down the hall into the kitchen. "That's gratitude for you," Diamond grumbled. "I haven't even eaten since yesterday, I been so busy running around, and Sharkey wants to dump me. The nerve. He lied and said you were unhappy with me, too."

Fifi brought out a tray of brownies. She nibbled, he wolfed down three.

"Red, as soon as Peter takes off for Baja, we can get together. I'll call you. I promise."

"You got to get over this hypnotism thing. You belong with Red Diamond, not with a dopey singer, three nymphos, and a trio of overmuscled gigolos."

He tried kissing her, but she avoided him.

"There's something bothering you, some secret. Spill it. You'll feel better."

Diamond noticed he was tapping out "Sing, Sing, Sing" on the kitchen table. He stopped and they continued to argue. He found himself singing "Don't Sit Under the Apple Tree." Then the room began to sway.

He was even hungrier and reached for another brownie.

"No more," she said, pushing his hand from the platter.

Her mouth was huge, a warm moist cavern he wanted to crawl into. He leaned forward and nearly toppled over.

"What's . . . going . . . on?"

"It's best this way, Red."

189

Fifi got up, but he couldn't get the energy to follow her. He rested his head on the table.

Waves rushed across him as a beach boy seized either arm and lugged him out the door. He lifted his legs playfully off the ground and let them carry him.

"Wheeeeeeeee!" he said.

"Be careful," Fifi said.

"We will," the biggest beach boy said, as the third member of the trio opened the door.

They came back in less than five minutes.

"Where is he?" Fifi demanded, spotting Diamond's .38 lying on an end table.

"The lady with gray hair said she'd take care of him," Biff said. "We met her on the way to the gate, near the stable."

The beach boys headed upstairs. Fifi grabbed the .38 and ran out the front door. In the distance, she could hear the Rottweilers barking.

Chapter Nineteen

Simon Jaffe was up a jacaranda tree, hanging on for dear life as four masses of black fur, muscle, and teeth snapped at him. He was seven feet off the ground, and the dogs' hydraulic-press mouths chomped only inches from him.

A beautiful woman strode into view carrying a long pool-cleaning pole.

"Lady, watch out. These dogs are killers," Jaffe said. He felt hung over and numb and strangely unafraid.

The woman grinned and walked in the dogs' midst. She raised the pole and began poking Jaffe.

"Hey!" he shouted, trying to protect his soft parts and still keep a solid grip on the tree trunk. He slipped and nearly fell. The dogs got more savage, jumping higher, barking louder.

The canine killers turned their attention from him when another woman came into view. A gorgeous blonde carrying a gun. The Rottweilers growled, unimpressed by her beauty or the weapon.

"Penelope! What are you doing here?" the pole carrier asked.

"Don't kill him, Ginger," the blonde said.

"Tomemas," Ginger bellowed, and the dogs froze. But they hungrily glared at Penelope.

The two women locked eyes hatefully. Jaffe watched the bizarre tableau from the tree. At times he was floating way above the hazy scene, sometimes he'd see it from one of the women's viewpoint, then he'd shift to a dog's perspective.

"The only reason I drugged him was to get him out without violence," Penelope said.

"I knew you didn't have it in you."

"Why him? What did he do?"

"He saved Piper," Ginger said. "He's a man, like the kind that ruined your sister."

"Not all of them are like that. Edwards wasn't."

"They're all the same. Get out of the way."

"That isn't why you killed Edwards. He had turned you down, hadn't he?" Penelope asked.

"You may be a Diana, but don't push your luck," Ginger hissed. "Put that gun down."

Penelope kept the weapon pointed at Ginger. "Call the dogs off."

"They could tear your pretty body to pieces before you got off one shot."

"Maybe, maybe not. But one shot is all it would take."

The women had forgotten about Jaffe, until they heard him humming "In the Mood" from his perch.

"You're willing to risk everything for that monkey?" Ginger asked.

"Call the dogs off," Penelope repeated.

After a long silence, Ginger ordered, "Uchi," and the dogs reluctantly returned to their kennel.

"You can rest assured the Dianas will hear about this," Ginger said before marching off."

"C'mon down, Red," Penelope said.

Moving cautiously and awkwardly, Jaffe slid down to earth. "Thanks, lady."

192

She threw her arms around him and pressed her warm body against his. "Oh Red, I'm so scared."

"Me too," he said, his voice aquiver.

She pulled away. "Did the dope freak you out? You're acting funny."

"You too. Considering we just met. Don't get me wrong, I don't mind."

She led him to the garage, learning from him that he was Simon Jaffe, a New York cabdriver. His clumsy movements were the result of his own natural lack of grace, and the dope in his system.

"Now if I can figure out how to pick up the Belt Parkway, I can get home," he said.

"You're in California."

"No shit. Excuse my French. I must've made a wrong turn somewhere. Is the meter running?"

"I better drive you," she said, as he stumbled over a sycamore root.

"All the way to Long Island? How do I explain this to Milly?"

She helped him into the car and he didn't resist. She checked his wallet and found business cards with "Red Diamond—Private Eye" and the Carlin Building address.

"I'll take you there," Penelope said. "Then I have to get back."

"Is my cab around here anywhere?"

"Just lean back and let me think," she told him as they headed down the long driveway.

"You're really pretty," Jaffe said, looking over at her as they got onto Sunset Boulevard.

"Be quiet, Red, please," she said.

"But my name's not Red."

"Shut up!" she yelled, fighting back tears. He cowered into the seat.

The usual assortment of freaks prowled Hollywood Boulevard as she parked the car and helped the still wobbly Jaffe out. A man with keys jangling like wind chimes hanging from his sombrero ranted about U.S. oppression. A preacher with clerical collar and Bermuda shorts warned of the dangers of sin. Break dancers performed while tourists clicked their pictures and had their wallets stolen.

"Hey, what's a fox like you doing with a jerk like this?" said a bouncy dude with a headband and single black leather glove.

Jaffe swayed on the sidewalk. "Why don't you leave us alone," he said timidly.

"You talkin' to me?" the dude asked, moving in menacingly close.

"I don't mean any offense."

"I don't care what you mean, fat ass. I'm gonna teach you a lesson, then me and the lady going to party, right, mama?"

Penelope took Diamond's .38 out of her purse. Her hand was rock steady as she pointed it in the dude's face. "Can you take a hint?" she asked.

The dude sped off like an Olympic track star.

"Boy, you sure are tough," Jaffe said admiringly as she put the gun back in her bag.

Penelope ran her hand over her face, took Jaffe's arm, and helped him into the building. She found his office number on the directory and led him upstairs. The light was on in his office. She drew the gun.

"Wait here," she ordered, leaning him against the wall.

"Maybe we better call the police," he whispered.

Adrenalined up, she ignored him and stalked down the corridor to his office. She threw the door open and aimed her gun at the figure inside.

"Hi, Da——oh, you're not my father. Who are you?"

Jaffe recognized the voice and staggered inside. "Sean. What are you doing out here?"

They set Jaffe on a couch, and soon he was in a stupor, not asleep, but not quite awake.

". . . Had brownies filled with opiated hash . . ."

"Dad? I never would've thought him the type."

". . . Accidental. He nearly was killed . . . I thought he was a tough private eye . . ."

". . . Delusional state . . . lived that way for two years . . . traumatic relapse . . ."

". . . Maybe when he wakes up he'll be . . . uncovered something bigger than he could imagine," the woman's voice said. ". . . His gun, but don't let him have it. He's liable to hurt someone."

". . . About you?"

"Forget me," she said.

The clouds got thicker and thicker and Jaffe drifted into a dark, slow-motion world.

The sun was shining as he awoke. He was in the bedroom of a well-kept, but not very well-furnished, apartment.

"Where am I?" he asked, hearing movement from the other room.

Sean came in. "You're in your apartment. You might be disoriented. I cleaned up a bit. You know how many empty beer cans you had lying around?"

"I don't drink much beer."

"Someone did. I got fifty-seven dollars over at the recycling plant for the old beer cans and whiskey bottles."

"Where's your mother?"

"You're Simon Jaffe?"

"Who did you expect, Mayor Koch?"

"You've got to think like a private eye. I've gotten some leads on this rock-and-roll assignment you gave me. Remember, finding out about Dickie Rogers, the first rock star who died?"

Jaffe got up and stretched. "Hoo boy, I feel like I slept for days. Did I miss the rush hour?"

"You're not driving a cab anymore."

"What?"

The exasperated youth led Jaffe out to the kitchen, put up coffee and buttered toast. He tried, unsuccessfully, to jog Jaffe's memory.

"I made an appointment to see Rogers's mother this morning," Sean said, sitting down at the table as Jaffe finished his breakfast. "I didn't realize you would be out of it. Now we'll never find Melonie."

"She's missing?"

"Yes. She's involved with these rock-and-roll people. You kept sending me off on tangents and I don't even know where you were, or the name of the lady who brought you home."

"Penelope?"

"Great. Penelope who?"

Jaffe scratched his head. "I don't think I caught her last name."

Sean covered his face with his hands.

"Don't feel bad, son. We'll find her."

As Jaffe drove east on the San Bernardino Freeway, he tried to make conversation.

"When we get back to New York, we'll go to shows and everything," he said. "You ever see Rodney Dangerfield?"

Sean shrugged.

"What a funny guy. 'I don't get no respect,' he says. But it's his face. What a kisser. You seen him? Isn't that a face?"

"Another twenty minutes and we'll be there. Don't you want to hear the background?"

"You'll have to ask the questions anyway. I never met this lady before."

"Neither did I, Dad."

"You sure she's willing to talk to us?"

"Yes, Dad. She said she'd talk, but not over the phone."

"This is quite a drive. I wonder what the fare would be."

Mary Lou Rogers's house was not quite a shack. The front yard featured a 1968 Chevy up on blocks, a pack of lazy dogs, and broken bottles hidden in foot-high crab grass. The roof was patched with a dozen different kinds of lumber, the paint on the sides was all but gone.

Mary Lou looked to be about a hundred and twenty, but moved like a woman half that age. It wasn't a tribute to her spryness, just that poverty had weathered her features worse than the siding. She was thin, with a craggy Okie face that might've once been pleasant. She rolled her own cigarettes as Jaffe and his son sat on the cat-scratched, dog-soiled sofa.

"My Dickie was the best there was," she said, lighting a cigarette that smelled like burning hair. "Elvis stole his style. Hank Williams heard my boy sing and said he was going to be great."

On the living room wall, above a black-and-white TV that flickered as a soap-opera couple went through a dramatic confrontation, was a framed platinum record.

"See that," she said, pointing to it and puffing on her foul smoke. "That was for 'Cuddly Baby.' You ever heard that?"

Sean tried to cut her off, but Jaffe said he hadn't heard the tune. She retrieved an album and put it on the turntable. A whiny voice sang, asking an unnamed girl to "Be my cuddly baby / No I don't mean maybe / Be my cuddly honey / We'll spend lots of money / You'll ride in my Nash / We'll spend all my cash / We'll be rolling in gravy / If you be my cuddly baby."

"Very nice," Jaffe said politely.

"You think that's good, get an earful of this," she said,

197

and the next song came on. They listened to both sides of the album, but were able to convince her they didn't need to hear it a second time.

Sean read the album jacket for clues but found none. Jaffe tried not to gag from the smell of the assorted wild life that wandered in and out through the torn screen door.

"Can you tell us about your son's death?" Sean asked.

"He was doing fine until he got in with that big-city crowd. He was a good boy. He had plans to take care of his mom when the money started coming in. Not like his no-good father who went off soon as Dickie was born. Or his brothers and sisters, who left as soon as they could. Dickie was good. Even as a child, the Reverend Watson said—"

"Excuse me," Sean interrupted. "But we're in a bit of a hurry. You were about to tell us—"

"What did the Reverend Watson say?" Jaffe asked curiously.

Mary Lou smiled at him and launched into a fifteen-minute account of Dickie's life that took them up to his being discovered singing at the San Bernardino County Fair at age seventeen.

"He started hanging out with a bad crowd. One night, his wicked ways caught up with him."

"I understand he was shot by a burglar," Sean said, becoming alert after nearly dozing off during the speech.

"That's what they say. But I don't believe it. I think one of his fancy gal friends did it."

"What makes you say that?" Sean asked.

"A mother can tell. Besides, my Dickie was a light sleeper. Like his pa, he always kept a loaded shotgun by the bed. No one coulda gotten in there unless he knew them."

"Is there anyone you suspected? Anyone who had a motive?" Sean asked.

"No one had a motive. He was the kindest boy you ever want to know. Handsome like a movie star. Want to see pictures?" She got up and headed for the photo album as Sean protested.

"I see his face on the record jacket. He's very nice. We don't need to see any others," Sean said.

"I'd like to see them," Jaffe said.

Sean shot him an annoyed look, and then Mary Lou was back with a six-inch-thick photo album. Sean sat back in his chair and stared at the cracked ceiling as Mary Lou repeated her detailed account of Dickie's life, this time with visuals.

"...At the fair when he was discovered. Look at that hair, isn't he cute?"

Dickie had enough grease on his head to lube a tractor. He had an insolent sneer and a guitar draped across bony shoulders.

"Looks like a nice boy."

"That's about the last picture took of him. The only other one I have is this." She slid an unmounted photo out of the book. "It was taken with some of them girls that began to hang around once he started to make money."

A more expensive guitar was draped around Rogers's neck. His chicken-bone arms encircled two girls and three others leaned against him.

Jaffe trembled as he looked at the picture.

"Are you coming down with something?" Mary Lou asked. "You shaking like you seen a spook."

"Dad, what is it?" Sean asked.

Jaffe pointed to the photo Mary Lou was holding. Sean studied it.

"The girl on the right, it could be Penelope," Sean speculated. "But that was so many years ago."

"The other one, next to her. It's Ginger."

"Ginger?"

"She tried to kill me yesterday. I remember that now. Penelope saved me."

"Land sakes," Mary Lou said.

"Penelope risked her life for me. And she's going back there."

"Where's there?" Sean asked.

Jaffe clenched his fists and pressed them against his head. "I can't remember."

Chapter Twenty

As they drove to Los Angeles, Jaffe racked his brain, trying to recall where he'd been. He had a vague memory of Penelope and Ginger fighting over something, snarling dogs, and an impressive mansion.

"The place reminded me of that show, 'Beverly Hillbillies,'" Jaffe said. "I guess you're too young to remember that. This backwoods fella, Jed Clampett, was out shooting, right, and his bullet drilled a hole and—"

"Try and concentrate on Penelope. She's probably in trouble," Sean said. "Do you recall any streets you might have been on?"

Jaffe squinted, clenched his teeth, and squeezed his fists as he struggled. "Amsterdam Avenue?"

Sean grabbed the Thomas Bros. map book and flipped quickly to the index. "No Amsterdam Avenue."

"Oh yeah, right, that's in New York. I once had a fare there that wanted to go to Jersey and wouldn't—"

"Penelope, Dad, remember Penelope?"

But Jaffe couldn't. They drove to Diamond's office. Sean rooted through papers, looking for a clue to where Jaffe/Diamond had been. He found the bill from the answering service, and got Jaffe to check for messages.

"You sound different today, Mr. Diamond," the woman at the service said. "Do you have a cold?"

"Uh, yeah. I guess that's it."

"Well, Mr. Moses Tartaglia called four times. He insisted it is urgent you call. Also a woman who would only give her name as Fifi said she loved you and goodbye."

"She didn't leave a number?"

"I'm afraid not. The operator did ask, but I'm afraid your caller disconnected."

"Thanks."

"I hope you and your girlfriend make up, Mr. Diamond."

"Yeah, well thanks again."

"She loves me," a confused Jaffe repeated several times after hanging up. "I guess I better call this Tartaglia in New York. Think whoever owns this office would mind if I make a long-distance call? I could pay him back."

"This is *your* office," Sean said.

"Oh."

"Anyway, he's just the attorney on your divorce from Mom."

"I don't want a divorce."

"The marriage is over. She thinks you're holding out money on her."

"Oh." Dejected, Jaffe sat on a worn chair while Sean continued to search the files.

"I better call this Tartaglia. You gotta be respectful of lawyers. They're smart and they can sue you easily."

Jaffe hesitated while Sean looked.

"Do you think it would be so bad if I called?" Jaffe asked.

Sean grunted. Jaffe took it as a grunt of approval. He dialed Tartaglia's number.

"I've been waiting to hear from you. Haven't you gotten my messages?" the lawyer asked.

"Uh, I've been busy. I'm sorry."

"What's the matter? You sound strange."

"Must be a cold."

"Two big news items. Becker died of a heart attack. He was intestate, which means his wife will get a substantial chunk of money."

"That's good news for Mrs. Becker."

"But more important, this Penelope Chance you told me about. I got suspicious when you said she was impersonating Fifi. I had an investigator check her out. I figure maybe Nichols had planted someone out there to trip you up."

"Penelope. Penelope Chance."

"Red, how sick are you?" he asked.

"I don't know."

"Anyway, this Penelope Chance, she went gonzo about fifteen years ago, right after her older sister got killed. She kicked around Haight-Ashbury, the East Village, Hollywood Boulevard. She has a few arrests for dope, disorderly conduct, assaulting an officer. She's been clean the past three years, involved with the Dianas."

"Where do I know that name from?"

"It's a counseling and support group for ex-offenders. Only women. They claim quite a success rate."

"Do you know where I could find her?"

"She has a house in Santa Monica, but she stays at Peter Piper's mansion when they're working."

"Piper. That's it. Where does he live?"

He read Jaffe the address.

"Thanks," Jaffe said, hanging up before the attorney could say anything more.

Sean hadn't listened in on the call. He was too wrapped up reading Diamond's case files.

"I think I know where Penelope is," Jaffe said.

Sean set down the file. "Great. Let's go."

As he drove, the route began to look familiar to Jaffe.

By the time he was turning off near Stone Canyon, he no longer needed to check the map book.

They pulled up to the gate and Jaffe spoke into the intercom. "Is Penelope here?"

"She's gone," a female voice said.

"How about Peter Piper?"

"He's gone too. Is that you, Mr. Diamond?"

"Uhh." Jaffe looked over questioningly at Sean, who nodded a quick assent. "Yes, it's me."

The automatic gate swung open.

"Boy, this is some place, isn't it?" Jaffe asked on the long drive from the front gate to the front door.

Babette was alone in the house, she said, explaining that Piper had decided he was under too much pressure. He was going to his Baja retreat with the beach-boy bodyguards to unwind.

Ginger and Penelope had accompanied them to Santa Monica Airport but would be staying in the city to take care of business.

"The album is going to be late," Babette said. "Penelope was very upset. Ginger stayed by her side the whole time."

"What time did they leave for the airport?" Sean asked urgently.

"About an hour ago. Why?"

Sean raced toward the door with Jaffe at his heels.

"A small plane. That's how thirty-one percent of the rock stars died," Sean said, hopping into the driver's seat. "Do you have the keys?"

"I drive. Slide over."

"We have to get there quick."

"Kid, you're looking at a man who once earned a fifty-buck tip by going from midtown to LaGuardia in fifteen minutes. Now slide over."

There was a hint of the Red Diamond confidence in the way Jaffe spoke and took the wheel. The ex-cabbie zoomed down the driveway, scraping the sides of the car when the gate took its time opening.

Jaffe cranked it up to fifty on city streets. "Are you sure you want to go along on this?" he asked. "It's not a fun ride. It's liable to be dangerous."

"I trust you, Dad."

Jaffe felt a warm glow. He didn't say anything, but as they screeched through turns and swerved to avoid other vehicles, he beamed.

When they got to the airport, they could see a Piper Cub starting to taxi out on the tarmac.

"That must be them," Sean shouted as they drove parallel to the cyclone fence that ringed the airport.

"I can't get to the entrance in time."

"They're gonna be killed. I know it," Sean said.

"Oh well then, here goes nothing." Jaffe spun the wheel and crashed through the fence. A section of it was held in place, stuck to the bumper.

They sped out on the asphalt runway, on a collision course with the Piper plane. The pilot saw them, but didn't have enough speed to take off. He tried an alternate path, but Jaffe compensated, and blocked his way.

The plane's propeller caught the edge of the fence and shattered, sending pieces of wire through the air at the speed of bullets. The crash knocked the wind out of Jaffe and his son.

The three bodyguards leaped from the small plane, which had fallen over on its side, with guns drawn. They spotted Jaffe and let out a collective groan.

"You again," Buzzy said.

"Now you've done it. It's a federal crime to interfere with a flight," Dean said.

"We're gonna make sure you don't ever cause trouble again," Biff added. "You're history, man."

The pilot, who had a slight cut on his forehead, came out yelling. "The plane. It's ruined. Ruined!"

"I think we're in trouble," Jaffe whispered to his son.

Piper popped out of the wrecked plane. "I was nearly killed." He saw Jaffe. "Red, what's going on?"

"He's the one behind this," Biff said, pointing to Jaffe with his gun. Sirens began getting closer.

"Why, Red, why?"

Jaffe turned to Sean.

Sean stepped forward. "Mr. Piper, my name is Sean Jaffe. I'm a fan of yours."

"I've been chased by autograph hounds but this is incredible," Piper said.

"I've studied the spate of deaths of rock-and-roll stars and have come to some startling conclusions. A significant percentage of rock stars die in small-plane crashes."

"I know that," Piper said. "My pilot checked the plane over this morning, and then Ginger did a double check."

"Ginger," Jaffe said.

"Mr. Piper, if you would have your mechanic go over the plane again," Sean said.

"There's no point. It's ruined," the pilot said. "It will never fly."

"Ginger's an ace mechanic," Biff said.

"Among other talents," Buzzy said.

"She's great," Dean piped up.

The bodyguards exchanged sheepish glances when they realized how vehement their unsolicited endorsements sounded.

"The police will be here soon," Sean said, as sirens got louder. Fire engines were already at the edge of the field. "Please."

Piper nodded and the pilot reluctantly opened the cowl. Fire trucks ringed the plane.

"What's this?" the pilot asked, spotting a pocketbook-sized object that didn't belong in the engine. He tugged.

"It's probably a bomb," Sean said.

206

The pilot fell back, dropping the object deep inside the engine.

Police cars raced up. Seeing the bodyguards' guns drawn, cops drew their own. Firemen held extinguishers, axes, and hose. Everyone was shouting and trying to take charge.

"There's a bomb in the plane," Jaffe said, in a voice that was more forceful than loud.

The cops and firemen who had been rushing forward retreated.

Two hours later, the bomb had been defused, and Piper, his bodyguards, the pilot, Jaffe and Sean debriefed.

It was a plastic explosive device, wired to the altimeter and designed to cripple the engine and controls when the plane reached ten thousand feet. The FAA inspector said there probably would've been no trace in the wreckage. The bomb technicians were admiring the handiwork. The police put out All Points Bulletins for Ginger and Penelope.

Piper called Sharkey, had the beach boys fired, and tried to rehire Diamond.

"You saved my life again. I'm going back to the studio to finish the album. With you as my bodyguard, I feel safer than ever."

"I can't take the job," Jaffe said, averting his eyes.

"But I'm dedicating my album to you. I've got three songs worked out already."

"I'm not the man you think I am," Jaffe said. He pointed to his son. "He deserves the credit. He figured it out."

"Don't be so modest, Dad. It was you who put me on the path, and you who drove here like it was the Indy 500."

"I don't care who did what. You're both hired. I'll hire your whole family."

"We have to find my sister first," Sean said.

"Your sister?" Piper asked.

"And Penelope," Jaffe said to Piper. "Maybe you could go into hiding for a day. Don't let anyone know where you are."

"But everyone knows what I look like."

"Cut your hair and get plain clothes," Jaffe said. "It's easy to confuse people if they're looking for certain characteristics. I think it was Phil Marlowe who was saying that's why bank robbers wear distracting hats."

"You're starting to remember the P.I. reading," Sean said happily.

"For whatever good it does," Jaffe said.

"I wish I knew where Penelope is," Jaffe said, standing with Sean at the top of Mulholland Drive, watching from the mountain crest as the sun set over Los Angeles.

"The police are looking for her," Sean said.

"But somehow this Penelope is real important to me. I don't understand why, but it's like, well, I don't know. You ever feel like you know you know something, but you can't quite put your finger on it?"

"No."

"I guess geniuses don't have problems like that," Jaffe said sincerely. "I never understood how I wound up with such a bright kid. Must be from your mother."

"I'm not a genius," Sean said. "Anyway, I learned as much from you as from Mom. If not more."

"I never got over a B in school. I dropped out my last year in high school. I had to get a job. My father, your grandfather, messed up his back on the loading dock. You don't want to hear this."

"I do, I do. We never talked about it."

"We never talked much. Lots of times I wanted to find out what it was like going to college," Jaffe said.

"You're smart, Pop, just not school-smart."

"It's funny, all this time we been talking, I keep thinking about one subject. Mythology, you know, with Zeus and Apollo and them gods and goddesses who was always changing people into animals."

"Maybe because of the name Penelope. It comes from Odysseus."

Jaffe scratched his chin. "Nah. Wait a minute. Diana. The huntress." He jumped from the fender of the car they'd been sitting on. "I remember. The mansion with the statues. C'mon."

The same luxury cars were parked outside. Jaffe experienced a blurry déjà vu as he sat in the car with Sean and stared at the house.

"The red Mercedes, that's Penelope's," Jaffe said.

"What do we do now?"

"We go in."

"But look at that gate. Who knows who is inside. Shouldn't we call the police?"

"You go for the cops. I'm going inside." Jaffe drew the .38 and held it awkwardly at his side.

"You shouldn't."

"I have to. For her. You go for help. Every second counts."

"Maybe I should come with—"

"Go," Jaffe ordered. He headed quickly for a clump of bushes.

He heard the car taking off as he slunk to the eight-foot-high stone fence. He scaled it quickly, almost wrenching his ankle tumbling down on the other side. He lay on the ground and waited. No one came. He edged toward the house.

The grounds were lushly landscaped with chest-high hedges, small fountains, and patches of brightly colored flowers. He lay in a bed of orange and white zinnias, hidden by a patch of bougainvillea, and caught his breath. He had never been so scared in his life.

Then he was up against the white colonial-style house with columns on the porches and green shutters on the windows. He crept around, peering in windows and checking out empty, lavishly furnished rooms. He saw no one until he'd nearly circled the building. There were four women gathered in the front parlor, seated in high-backed wooden chairs. They ranged in age from late twenties to early fifties. Ginger sat at the head of the table.

She was talking angrily. Jaffe couldn't hear what she was saying. He didn't see Penelope.

He went to the front porch and tried the door. It opened without a creak. He padded upstairs, holding his breath and his gun.

He found her in the second room, tied to the headboard of a big brass bed. She saw him and her eyes went wide. He made a shhhing gesture, but there was no need. She was gagged.

He shut the door behind himself and went to the bed. He set the gun down and fumbled with the knots.

"Mmmmntmg," she said.

"Sorry," he said, and gently peeled the tape from her mouth.

"What are you doing here?"

"Uh, I came to get you out."

"You'll be killed."

"Don't worry. I sent my son for help."

His fingers refused to work from a mixture of fear and being so close to the most beautiful woman he'd ever seen.

"There's a scissors in the dresser," she said.

He got a small manicuring kit and began slicing the bonds. Midway through, Penelope stiffened.

"Sorry. Did I cut you?"

"What a touching scene," Ginger sneered from the doorway, an ugly Beretta in her hands. Behind her stood the other women. Two held guns.

Jaffe dropped the manicuring kit on the bed.

"How did you get here?" one of the women demanded.

"Uh, I, uh, just came in," Jaffe said, trying to control the quiver in his voice. "The police are coming. You better give up."

"Hah!" Ginger said, snatching his gun. "I've heard that line before. Tie him up."

One woman took the scissors from him and bound him roughly. Another retied Penelope.

"We can arrange a lovers' quarrel. A fatal one, with fireworks," Ginger smirked, before leading the group downstairs.

"You were very brave. Too bad it was in vain," Penelope whispered.

"Why? Why do they have to kill us?"

"It's a long story. I wish I had told you everything. I wish you had listened to me and gone away. I wish, I wish . . ." Her voice trailed off.

"This is nuts," Jaffe said, sweating profusely. "Where are those cops? I never figured on being killed by a gang of crazy women."

"I love you, Red," Penelope said, twisting in her bonds to kiss him. "I only wish things had worked out."

Jaffe barely felt her lips. He was dizzy with terror. He opened and closed his eyes several times, hoping to wake up anywhere else. Preferably in his basement, reading a pulp magazine or dime detective novel.

"This reminds me of the time Red and Fifi were trapped in the manicurist's parlor Rocco was using as a cover for his espionage operation," he said when he finally regained a small part of his composure. "See if you can

211

wiggle a bit and get that manicuring kit from the other side of the bed."

Penelope wiggled her buttocks to move the kit over. Despite the imminent danger, or maybe because of it, he found himself more aroused than he ever imagined.

"Would you at least tell me why we're going to get killed?"

While Penelope writhed on the bed next to him, she said, "Ginger was one of the first groupies. A singer named Dickie Rogers treated her badly and she killed him. It was like a shark tasting blood."

The fabric of Penelope's clothes stretched and strained, and Jaffe found it hard to concentrate.

"Ginger drifted around the rock-and-roll world. She found groupies who had been abused, or thought they'd been abused. Some were jilted lovers, some were just psycho. They've been killing rock stars for twenty-five years!"

"What about you?" he managed to ask.

"My sister was one of them." There were tears in her eyes. "She died in an explosion. At first I believed the story Ginger put out, that she was doing effects for a band that didn't take safety precautions. She was so special.

"Last year I found out she was one of the Dianas. I was intrigued. Because she had been a member, I was able to infiltrate them.

"I discovered the real story. My sweet sister had been making a bomb when she died. They'd poisoned her mind, turned her into a killer groupie.

"I decided I was going to stop this insanity. I went to Edwards to warn him, so we could catch a Diana in the act. He didn't believe me. Then Ginger got suspicious."

A final bump and grind, and the kit came into view. Jaffe rolled over and tried to open it with his teeth, his face inches from her thigh.

"What tipped her off?" he asked. He got the nail file

between his teeth and began sawing the rope. He leaned against her for support.

"I fell in love with you," she said, and he nearly swallowed the file.

"Me?" he mumbled through pursed lips.

"You. You're hokey, with outdated chivalry and macho and all the things I made fun of. But you have something you believe in, that you stick to at all costs. You're wacky, but otherwise you couldn't do what you do."

He bobbed his head sawing.

"Ginger got on to me when I wouldn't let the dogs tear you apart. She's kill-crazy."

Penelope flexed her arms and the ropes split. She quickly untied his hands.

"They've been discussing the best way to kill me, to get mileage out of it," she said as they hopped unbound from the bed. "I'm so scared. There's no limit to what Ginger will do."

His head spun as he glanced around the room. The window was barred with security gates and there was no phone.

"Think, think, think, think," he mumbled to himself. "Let's put the dresser against the door," he finally said, pulling at the six-foot-high bureau.

The legs scraped noisily on the floor. The low mumble of discussion they had heard from downstairs stopped. They shoved the bureau until it leaned against the door, then frantically piled up the bed, armchairs, and night table.

There was the sound of high-heeled feet hurrying up the stairs.

Chapter Twenty-one

"**O**pen up," Ginger demanded.

"Or you'll huff and you'll puff and you'll blow our house down," Jaffe said. His voice started as Diamond's, but cracked back into Jaffe's in the middle of the sentence.

Bullets ripped through the door and the thick bureau, smashing into the walls above their heads.

"Maybe we should," Penelope said.

"They're going to kill us anyway." Lying on the floor, he took her in his arms and they melted into each other, oblivious to the gunshots and the rattling at the door.

"This is the police. We know you're in there. Come on out with your hands up," a bullhorn-bolstered voice boomed from outside.

The shooting stopped and Jaffe could hear the Dianas scurrying about. He duck-walked to the window. An army of cops had assembled on the lawn. A SWAT team officer was standing with the bullhorn, half-hidden behind one of the statues of Diana.

Jaffe crawled back to Penelope. "Now where were we?"

"What should we do?"

"Nothing. Let the gals surrender, and then we can

214

walk out like it was the Easter parade." They resumed their embrace.

There was a shot. Then a few more.

"Idiots!" Jaffe said, getting up and crawling back to the window. "They're trying to shoot it out."

"It's worse than you think. They store explosives and incendiary devices downstairs."

The police let off a few rounds. A woman cried out, and more shots were fired from the house.

"You've got thirty seconds," the cop with the bullhorn said. He was answered with a volley.

There was a hurried tread on the stairs and Ginger was at the door. "I'll get you. This is your fault," she shouted, throwing herself against the door with a maniacal determination. The furniture fort Jaffe and Chance had built tumbled, and Ginger stormed into the room.

She aimed at Jaffe. "You ruined it. You *man,* you!"

Penelope dove at Ginger in the millisecond before she pulled the trigger. The bullet meant for Jaffe tore into Penelope's body.

The window shattered and a tear-gas can fell into the room as Jaffe lunged for the stunned Ginger. She had a fanatic's strength as they grappled. Unable to aim at him, she battered his neck and torso with the pistol.

The room filled with tear gas. They choked. The drapes caught on fire. Black smoke mixed with the tear-gas cloud.

Jaffe had the gun in his hand. Ginger raked at his face with nails like bear claws. He squeezed the trigger and the clawing stopped. She fell away from him.

He kept thinking what Mike Hammer had said about shooting a truly evil woman: it was easy.

The smoke and gas tore his lungs. He crawled along the floor, desperately feeling for Penelope. He heard her moan and made his way to her side.

She coughed, and blood trickled from the corner of her mouth.

"Oh, Red," she said as he took her in his arms.

"Don't say anything. Save your strength."

"I'm not going to make it."

"You will."

"Tell me you love me."

"I love you."

"You used to say it differently," she gasped, after a fit of body-shaking coughs.

"I love you, angel. Don't give up," he said. The tears flowing down his face were only partly from the gas.

He lifted her and staggered through the cloud. He stumbled on the stairs, and nearly dropped her. Flames touched him and he cried out. Penelope didn't, even when the fire wrapped red-hot tentacles around her leg.

He made it to the door and yanked it open, holding her in his arms.

"Hold your fire! Hold your fire!" the SWAT commander ordered as he saw him appear.

In the last second before he collapsed, he managed to twist so his lady love fell on top of his body, and not the unforgiving ground.

Where could they have taken her?

I hit every hangout and hideout in town with no luck.

Then I called my buddy, Detective Tom Dunne, and he made sure that every cop and stoolie in the city knew there was a crisp sawbuck for the first gazebo to spot my baby.

"I'm starting to get a bad feeling about this whole shebang," I told him, lighting one smoke off the dying end of the other. "You got Rocco's prints on file?"

"In a special safe," Dunne said.

"Let's go to the morgue."

We had them wheel Rocco out, and took prints off his hands.

216

"*Look at this,*" Dunne said, *holding up the print card next to his file card.* "*They ain't even close.*"

I bent over the stiff. Around his eyes and near his ears, I saw small surgical scars.

"*I killed Rocco's double,*" I said. "*Plastic surgery.*"

"*Tough break,*" Dunne said. "*What are you gonna do?*"

"*What do you think?*"

"Dad? Dad? Can you hear me?"

"I can hear you but don't call me Dad," Diamond said. Or tried to say. His voice sounded like a bullfrog with laryngitis. He was lying in a hospital burn ward, with bandages covering his legs, hands, and face. "What happened?"

"You got burned in a fire. The police tear-gas grenades set off explosives stored in the house. You've been out of it for two days."

"Fifi?" he asked, trying to sit up.

"She's in critical. The two of you were the only survivors."

"Ginger's dead?"

"They couldn't say for sure. They're trying to match up dental records," Sean said. "I guess I'll stay here with you. I've given up on finding Melonie."

"If there's one thing you gotta learn, kid, it's that it ain't over 'til it's over."

Diamond sat by Fifi's bed, like a faithful hound at his master's grave. A wall full of state-of-the-art machines was the only barrier between her and the big sleep. She was swathed in bandages, in a coma.

The P.I. felt helpless. His fists and his gun were useless; Fifi's life was in others' hands.

"You're not doing anyone any good sitting there day and night," the nurse said after finding him sleeping in a chair in Fifi's room.

"She might need me."

A doctor tried to order him back to bed. Diamond whipped his gun out from under his hospital smock. "Did Rocco send you?" he demanded.

The doctor retreated, yelling for hospital security.

Peter Piper used his financial clout to smooth matters over, and Diamond was permitted to maintain his vigil. It was arranged that he share the room with his love. He watched the various tubes and wires that kept her going, dreading each second that they might stutter.

It happened in the early morning hours. Red was dozing. There was a gurgling noise, and he was instantly awake.

He stood over Fifi. Her eyes fluttered, then opened.

"Red?" she said in a ghastly parody of her old voice.

"The one and only. I knew you had too much heart to die," he said. "I got a single question."

"What is it?"

"Will you marry me?"

Tears trickled down her face. "Yes."

He turned away before she could see his matching waterworks.

"You been good to me, Piper, and I appreciate it," Diamond said.

"I wouldn't be around to do anybody favors if it hadn't been for you. It's given me a whole new perspective on things."

"Letting Sean stay at your hacienda, and footing the medical bills for me and my doll is a classy bit of business," Diamond said.

Piper dismissed the praise with a shoving-aside gesture.

"I need another favor," Diamond said.

"Just ask."

"Sean has a picture of his sister. I need you to put out the word with your friends. I'm trying to reach Goodfellow.

218

I think he's gone to ground with her. Can you get the pix duped and have it shown around on the QT?"

"Roger wilco," Piper said.

"Don't let Goodfellow get tipped. If you could offer a few bucks reward for the girl's location, it would help."

"Would ten thousand do?"

"Perfectly. And don't let Sean know about it. The dumb kid's liable to go off and put the kablooie on the whole deal."

"Hush hush," Piper said, touching his lips. "What happens when we find her?"

"I'll handle it."

As soon as Piper was gone, Fifi spoke up. "Red, what are you going to do?"

"Whatever has to be done, cupcake."

"What's that mean?"

"To make an omelet you have to scramble a few yeggs."

"Please stop talking like that," she pleaded. "And promise me you'll let the police handle it."

"Take it easy, Fifi honey. That's advice from the doctor."

She winced as she sat up in bed. "This isn't going to work. You can pretend whatever you want. I've been doing a lot of thinking. I'm Penelope Chance, not Fifi La Roach."

"That's Roche, not Roach."

"Whoever. Maybe if you got counseling, we could work it out. Your fantasy isn't enough for the two of us to live in."

"I love when you talk poetry."

"Red, I'm serious. Or maybe I should call you Simon."

"You're just under the influence of drugs. The docs are pumping you full of—"

"That's your screwy idea. I'm fine."

"I'll still love you. Even if you never get back the way you were."

219

"If you love me, you will let the police handle the problem. Plus you'll go to a psychiatrist."

Diamond lit a cigarette. "The kid needs my help. His sister, too. I'm close to Rocco, I can feel it. You got to understand, I can't quit now."

"This isn't going to work," she said, rolling over and facing the wall.

So I wore out shoe leather going from block to block, town to town. Knocking on doorbells, knocking on heads, trying to get a lead on her. It was as if the earth had swallowed her up.

When I heard any one of a dozen songs, or smelled Shalimar, or saw a certain shade of blond hair being tossed by the wind, it hit me in the heart like a Joe Louis hook.

Then I ran into Moses Tartaglia. He's a lawyer, but I don't hold it against him. He got me looking into Sid Becker, a well-known conniver who hustles all the angles.

Somehow the trail led me to L.A., to a sound studio where Glenn Miller was making sweet music. Fifi was there, but the hypnosis was still playing marezy doats with her skull. She had gotten hooked up with a clatch of nutty dames . . .

Piper came in followed by a petite Oriental girl. She peered around timidly while Piper spoke.

"It's been very exciting. Lots of people have responded. Several even claimed to be the girl in the photo. But this lady's story is the most promising. Tell him, Jennie."

"Is the offer legit?" Jennie asked in a voice that reminded Diamond of Judy Holliday.

He nodded.

"I know Melonie. She's a troublemaker. Ralph's got her working in a fleabag in Hollywood as punishment for trying to run away."

"Where is it?"

"Will I get paid?"

"If she's there."

"She was, at least she was there yesterday."

"You take me there."

"No way. He'd kill me if he knew. One girl snitched him to the cops once. They found her body in the Angeles Forest. She had been tortured. Of course the pigs never proved anything. Ralph's too smart. At least he used to be. He's gotten weird recently."

Diamond thought of Melonie in his clutches. "Gimme the address."

Jennie did. "I'm gonna get paid, right?"

Diamond signaled Piper, who took out his checkbook.

"A check?" she complained. "I only deal in cash."

"Bring it to my bank," Piper said.

Grumbling, she accepted the paper. "If this bounces, I'll get your ass, believe me." She strode from the room.

"Quite a young lady," Piper said, grinning. "Now what happens?"

Diamond began dressing. "I take care of business, and then me and Fifi get married."

"No we don't," Fifi said.

"What?" Diamond asked.

"My name is not Fifi. You are not a super-hero detective. I will not spend my life waiting for you to be killed while you run around playing make-believe. If you go now, it's over. Forever."

"I can call the police and—" Piper began.

"No! Red Diamond does not let the flatfeet do the dirty work for him. This is my case and my daugh——daugh— —daugh——Melonie. A man's gotta do what a man's gotta do."

"Not true!" Fifi said. "Society would collapse in a day if everyone followed your rules."

"It would fall apart even quicker if there wasn't mukaluks like me willing to stick our necks out."

221

Dressed, Diamond slid the .38 out from under his pillow. He handed it to her.

"You remember how to use this from the time—"

She threw the gun back on his bed. "Stop it! Stop it right now. You're going to get killed."

Diamond picked up the gun and handed it to Piper. "You know how to use this?"

"Point it at the bad guys and pull the trigger?"

"That'll have to do. She's not seeing things straight. She's still under the influence. She should be safe. I've got Rocco on the run. But you take care of her, hear?"

"Red, perhaps she's right," Piper said, holding the weapon uneasily.

"Life ain't worth living if you don't risk it every now and then."

Fifi was crying as he walked out.

Chapter Twenty-two

The address was for the No Tell Motel, a ten-room dive with bars on the windows and a stagnant swimming pool. The green fungus in the pool matched the stucco walls. The sign out front flashed on and off. It boasted: VACANCY . . . PHONES IN MOST ROOMS . . . WATERBEDS . . . ADULT CABLE. WE HAVE AIR-CONDITIONING.

If there was air-conditioning in the office, it wasn't working. The man behind the counter had sweat stains the same color as the pool fungus under his scrawny arms. He looked like an ex-sailor who had been marinated in brine for at least half of his sixty years.

"I'm just in from out of town," Diamond said, putting on his best yokel voice. "A friend told me this is the place to get action."

"You look like a cop to me," the night manager said.

Diamond took three hundred dollars out of his wallet. "I'm in town for one night. If this ain't the spot to spend my cash, you let me know."

The night manager stared at the money like he'd never seen it before. "Maybe I can help."

"My friend, Fred, you must know Fred, he told me there's a sweet little brown-haired chickie here. Curly hair, kinda thin."

"I know the one. Any arrangements you work out with her is strictly your business. But there's a fifty-dollar guest fee."

Diamond counted out five tens and the night manager scooped them up. "Room Twelve."

The P.I. hurried out.

Room Twelve was on the second floor, facing the pool. He knocked at the flimsy door. The curtain parted. He held the money up, partially blocking his face.

Four locks were unlatched and a cloud of cigarette smoke escaped as the door opened. He stepped into the darkened room.

"Oh my God!" Melonie said.

She was skinnier than in the photo, with dark rings under her eyes. She was wearing black bikini briefs and a bra with nipple cutouts. She covered her face, and then tried to cover her body. She dropped the cigarette she'd been puffing.

Diamond picked it up and drowned it in her beer can. He jerked the soiled blanket from the much-used bed and handed it to her. She wrapped herself in it.

"Dad. What are you doing here?"

"The name's Red Diamond. Your brother and I have been tracking you. I'm here to get you out." The P.I. felt a trembling in his hands. He decided it was because he was still getting over his injuries from the fire.

He looked around. Besides the bed there was a battered dresser, a plastic folding chair, a night table, and a lamp. All of the furniture would have been rejected by the Salvation Army. The only new item in the bleak room was a large clock, which faced the bed.

"I can't go," she said in an emotionless monotone. "He'll kill me."

"If you want, I will get you out."

She sat on the bed. "You can't help me, Dad. It's too late. I used to think there was a way out. All it got me was

224

this." She exposed her back, which bore an "R" burned into her flesh.

"How'd you get that?"

"With a hot hanger. Ralph told me if I wasn't good enough for his A-team, I would still earn him money as a flatbacker." She sniffled. "Do you have any cocaine? Or uppers?"

He shook his head.

"Downs? Smack? Booze?"

"Are you hooked?"

"No," she said, and broke down in tears. "I just need something to take the edge off."

She began talking as if he wasn't there. "It wasn't so bad at first. Ralph loved me. He took me to parties. Then he made me ball his friends. For money. It wasn't Ralph's fault. He was doing more and more coke. He got different. But he still loves me. Even when he beats me, it's only 'cause he loves me. If only I can earn enough, I know he'll forgive me. Deep down inside."

Diamond removed his jacket and draped it over her shoulders. He stood next to the door, arms folded, looking at the pathetic little girl.

"You better get out of here," she said, angry at his pitying glance. "Ralph's got a gun and he's super-mean."

The door flew open and a gun-waving masked man charged in. "Stick 'em up, fucker! Move and I'll—"

He had expected to find Diamond and the girl in bed, and Diamond's being only a couple of steps away from the door threw off his rhythm.

Before he had a chance to say any more, Diamond tackled him. Melonie began a rising and falling wail that didn't correspond to who was on top or bottom.

Diamond slammed his fists into the masked figure, who tried to bite him. The P.I. managed to pull the bandit's mask up so it covered his eyes and pound a half-dozen solid shots into his face and stomach.

His mask dropped and the gun fell.

"Ralph!" Melonie shouted.

"Rocco!" Diamond growled.

They punched and kicked at each other, tumbling across the mildewed carpet, banging into furniture. Melonie continued to scream like an ambulance going off a cliff.

Diamond got an elbow into Rocco's floating ribs, and the pimp rolled back. Red was finally able to seize the pimp's gun.

"You wouldn't shoot an unarmed man, would you?" Rocco sniveled.

Red answered by squeezing the trigger six times. Rocco didn't know about the last five. The first one went through his forehead and into his brain.

Melonie's screams trailed off and police car sirens picked up the wail. Car doors slammed in the motel parking lot.

"I've never seen a more open-and-shut case of justifiable homicide," Tartaglia said as he and Diamond walked down the courthouse steps.

"But you didn't even tell the D.A. it was Rocco," Diamond said.

"I didn't need to. An outraged father, a pimp playing the badger game killed with his own weapon. I'm amazed they even held you the week."

"But the D.A. oughta know. It's gonna affect crimes all over Los Angeles, all over the world."

"I promise I'll mention it to him next time I see him. You've got to understand this Rocco business doesn't show up in any records. It might make the prosecutor nervous. He could push for competency hearings."

"Competency? You mean like fruitcake stuff? Maybe the D.A. was on Rocco's pad. Do you think—"

"Trust me, Red. I got you out, didn't I?"

They had reached the parking lot. Tartaglia walked to the side of a bus.

"Where's your car?" Diamond asked.

"I borrowed this from a friend."

Tartaglia banged on the side and the door hissed open. "Surprise!"

The bus was from Peter Piper's tour. Diamond and Tartaglia climbed aboard to join Sharkey, Piper, Nita, Babette, Sean, and Melonie. While Nita drove west, Babette served champagne.

"I want you to hear this," Piper said, turning on a tape player. Through hidden speakers, his voice, with musical accompaniment, blasted out.

> *Things got dark,*
> *Problems was piling,*
> *Along came Diamond,*
> *Now I'm smiling.*
> *He don't take crap,*
> *He's nobody's fool.*
> *He's forties tough,*
> *And eighties cool.*

Diamond smiled, the others cheered. Melonie came and sat next to him. "Sean told me about your searching for me," she said. "All the dangers you ran into."

"He was busted up about your leaving."

"Really? But *you* saved my life. I'm sorry Ross had to die."

"Ralph killed him?"

She nodded. "That's what he told me. He said Ross was snooping in my business and he was gonna teach him a lesson. You have to believe me, Ralph wasn't that evil when I first met him. I'm glad you and Sean came when you did." She leaned over and awkwardly planted a kiss on Diamond's cheek.

227

"What about that bull that Ralph loves you?"

"My shrink taught me about the Stockholm syndrome. I was like Patty Hearst, he said. Peter recommended me to him. Do you believe it, the doc gets three hundred for a fifty-minute hour? Peter is paying it. He's gonna help me get my career started. I didn't even have to boff him. Ain't that great, Dad?"

"Uh-huh," Diamond said, staring out the window and hoping he'd see a red Mercedes. During his week in the slammer, Fifi hadn't visited. He'd heard from Piper that she'd been released from the hospital. Piper tried getting in touch with her for Diamond, but she had moved out of her house.

Sharkey plopped down in the seat Melonie had vacated.

"So, how's about a long-term contract? You'll handle the biggest names in the rock biz. Go on world tours, make lots of money, get your name in the paper."

"Sounds great to me," Tartaglia said, as he breezed by with a bottle of bubbly. He leaned over Diamond. "I only wish we hadn't snuck you out before the press could get wind of it. The courthouse-step interviews are great for business. Do you think it would be poor form to throw a press conference at the mansion?"

"Talk to Peter."

"I'm thinking of moving out here. I am licensed in California and New York. Remember what Horace Greeley said." He turned to Sharkey. "I've got ideas to improve recording contracts. A guaranteed way to get the latest singles on major radio station playlists. Are you interested?"

"I could be," Sharkey said.

"Let's go to lunch and talk about a retainer," Tartaglia said, warmly slapping Sharkey's shoulder and inadvertently spilling champagne.

"The first thing you ought to do is get rid of Kirk," Diamond said in a monotone.

"I told you, he gets things done," Sharkey said.

"He's stealing from artists, bootlegging his own records to rip off royalties."

"That bastard! My accountants suspected something funny. Can you prove it? That cuts into my percentage. I'll kill him."

Diamond shrugged. "Maybe I can get someone to come forward. I'll see."

"Super, super," Sharkey said. "I'm not leaving this town until I have you tied up in a long-term personal-service contract."

"As Mr. Diamond's attorney, I must say I'm sure we can work out something mutually advantageous," Tartaglia interjected. "About that lunch—"

Diamond's attention drifted to where Sean, Melonie, and Piper stood at the front of the bus. Melonie and Piper were holding hands, very tentatively, in an innocent manner that belied both of their bedroom backgrounds. There seemed to be genuine affection between the two, and he gave her hand a little squeeze as they parted.

The lawyer led the promoter away, bending his ear about "adhesion contracts that set a bad precedent."

Sean and Piper came over. "Your son has some fantastic concepts. I'm going to hire him as my right-hand man. As soon as he gets out of school."

"If it's okay with you, Dad——I mean Red?"

"It's your own business."

"Thanks. Peter even offered to pay my way for an MBA at Harvard Business School. Assuming I get admitted."

"With your grades, you're being too modest," Piper said.

"Peter, I'd like to talk with you. In private," Diamond

said. Sean nodded, and went back to his sister. Piper sat close to Diamond and cocked his head, making it clear he would hang on the P.I.'s every word.

"It's real nice of you to be spending all this money on those two kids. But don't overwhelm them. Or take advantage of them. They both got lots of vulnerabilities. If I ever found out you were using them—"

"Red, please, I like them. Even if they weren't your kids"—Piper saw the befuddled expression on Diamond's face—"which they aren't necessarily. I mean the money I spend putting Melonie back on her feet or schooling Sean is petty cash."

"To you, not them. I don't want to see them spoiled. Or get used to something and then have the rug pulled out."

Piper affectionately punched Diamond's arm, then gulped when he realized what he had done. "Sorry, but I just wanted to say, you're one hell of a great guy."

Diamond smiled. "Thanks. For all of us. I know you'll do the right thing. I just got a lot on my mind."

"Penelope—uh, Fifi?"

Diamond nodded.

"As someone who has had more failed love affairs in a year than most men have in a lifetime, let me tell you, things do tend to work out. You know, that's not a bad idea for a song." Moved by his Muse, Piper hurried to the front of the bus and scribbled lyrics on a sheet of paper.

Diamond stared out the window. On a bus full of happy people, he was alone with his thoughts.

Could Goodfellow have been a lookalike? Maybe the D.A. knew something he wasn't telling. Maybe Rocco wasn't dead and had kidnapped Fifi, using hypnosis to spirit her away. So close, only to have her slip through his fingers again. Was that his fate, to never be united with the woman he loved?

They rode down Sunset Boulevard through the many faces of Los Angeles. Hispanic barrios with gang-graffitied walls, the middle-class neighborhoods with overpriced houses on palm-tree-lined streets, out to the ritzy enclaves of Piper's neighborhood, the baronial B's, Beverly Hills, Bel Air, Brentwood.

The bus rolled into Piper's estate and pulled up in front of his house.

Diamond saw the red coupé. He bounded from the bus, racing around the grounds until he found her, seated on a bench, with the hint of lilacs in the air.

"Fifi!" he yelled. He ran and threw his arms around her. She didn't respond.

"Red, you can pretend to be whoever you want. My name is Penelope Chance. Can you accept that?"

"If you say so."

"Fine. We have a lot of learning to do about each other. I'm not the woman of your fantasies."

"But you are."

"No! If you can't accept me the way I am, I can say goodbye now. I came back because I thought it was crummy disappearing while you were in jail."

"I understand."

"Do you?"

"Maybe."

"I felt bad about that scene in the hospital. I want to change you, but I don't want you to change. It's very peculiar."

Red stopped himself before he said it was the hypnotism.

"Do you want to make a go of it?" she continued. "I won't try and make you into Simon Jaffe, but you can't try and make me into Fifi La Roche."

He took her in his arms. "I love you, Fi——uh, Penelope."

"Red, when we're alone . . ." she whispered in his ear.

"Yes?"

"Call me Fifi."